The Magick of Merlin

Modern Magick, 10

Charlotte E. English

1

I could tell you just how much the Elvyng family, in the person of William Elvyng (Crystobel's father), had paid for Merlin's Grimoire back in the eighties. I could also tell you how much the spell-book had been valued at, about eight years ago.

Believe me, you don't want to know.

You'd spit chips. Like I did.

'*How* do people get so wealthy?' I complained to Val, as I sat one morning in the library at Home, perusing the Elvyngs' photos and documents pertaining to the impossible spell-book.

'The argent operation can't hurt,' she said, without looking up from her laptop. 'And you've seen the prices at the Emporium.'

Right. If you happen to be the only family in the country with a secret supply of the most important magickal substance known to man, and therefore sole rights to stock a shop with souped-up magickal artefacts, you *would* be rolling in it.

History had rather favoured the Elvyngs.

I sighed.

Val looked up, and directed at me the Quizzical Brow. 'Suffering some envy?'

'Aren't you?'

Val shrugged. 'What would you even do with that kind of wealth, if you had it?'

'Well, I...' I had to pause, and think about it. I could live in my own personal castle, with a swarm of servants to wait upon me hand and foot. I could have a private plane, and go anywhere I liked. I could eat every day at the finest, Michelin-starred restaurants in the country.

None of which sounded much like me.

'I'd become the Society's secret benefactor,' I decided. 'Oodles of funding, every year, and nobody would know where it came from.'

'Like Ancestria Magicka.'

I grimaced. 'Right.'

'It's too bad you've just told me, then, isn't it? Cover blown.'

I sniffed. 'You would never give away my secrets.'

'Not without handsome compensation, anyway.' Val missed the wounded look I sent her, having returned her attention to her laptop. Presumably she was still deep in the magickal dark web, scouring the online world for any mention of lucrative book heists, or the sale of improbably expensive grimoires.

I went back to Crystobel's documents. I'd already lingered a long time over her photos of the grimoire itself, torn between wonder and horror. The book was old, and by that I mean *old.* Hand-stitched bindings, scrubby leather covers, crumbling pages — the works.

So far, so convincing.

I may have been a little disappointed at how ugly it was. I was definitely disappointed by its poor condition. Didn't people know to take *care* of priceless artefacts?

My mind drifted back to the book-box that had stolen Jay's heart, back when we'd (unwisely) paid a visit to the Elvyng Emporium. The box was enchanted; slowly, gradually, anything placed in it would be restored to a better condition, some of the deleterious effects of time reversed. I had no doubt the Elvyngs would have kept Merlin's Grimoire in just such a box, which suggested it had reached them in a still worse state.

Merlin would've been crushed.

If there ever was a Merlin.

On this point, I remained profoundly sceptical. Merlin was a myth. Besides, while his purported grimoire was scarily old, it still wasn't old enough. As near as anyone can determine, a hypothetical real Merlin would have lived something like fifteen hundred years ago, and possibly rather more; surely no book, however magickal, could have survived in legible condition for so long?

But all this might be immaterial. Crystobel had said, *I am less concerned with the precise identity of the book's author than I am with the contents.* Whoever had written it, the grimoire contained charms and enchantments the likes of which most of us would kill for. That's why the Elvyngs wanted it back — at almost any price.

'Surely,' I said aloud, struck by a sudden thought, 'they'd have copies of every page.'

Val looked up, frowning. 'What?'

'Of the grimoire. The Elvyngs, I mean. Why do they need it back so badly? They wouldn't be so careless as to keep only one source of such important magicks. They would have records. Photos. Transcriptions.'

'No doubt, but now they also have competition. Potentially, someone else could be using all that secret magick.' She blinked sightlessly at me. 'That's a good point, Ves.'

'What point did I make?'

'Whoever stole the book. Did they just want to own it because it's valuable, or did they want to use it?'

'Both?' I ventured.

'Maybe. Maybe not. Anyone suddenly coming out with copies of magicks only the Elvyng family have been able to produce would attract a certain attention, no?'

'If it were known. The thieves could be out there, working marvels in secret.'

'So they could. The question remains: was it the book itself that was wanted, or was it something *in* the book that was important? A charm or something, that the Elvyngs wouldn't share?'

'Good questions all, Val, but I don't see how they can be answered until we find the thieves.'

She sighed, and her mind came back from wherever it had gone. 'Probably not. Still, it's something else to search for. Accounts of unusual feats performed by unlikely parties.'

The laptop once again swallowed her attention whole.

I stared, a little hopelessly, at my pile of papers. I'd covered the desk in them. I had not only Crystobel's documents, but sheaves of print-outs I'd squirreled up from all over the internet. Every mention I could find of the Elvyng family's doings for the past several years (lots of attending-of-events and sightings-at-magickal-libraries, plus the various accomplishments of the individual family members, and the doings of their prestigious academy). Val had been hoping for reports of bad blood between them and someone else — another family, or organisation. Something.

No luck. They were perfect. Everyone loved them.

I had also struck out on the subject of Merlin's Grimoire in the media, in that there was almost no mention of such a thing. Ever. All I'd been able to dig up was scant reference to the auction at which William Elvyng had purchased the book, and the account consisted of exactly three lines: a minimal description of the book, its purported provenance, and to whom it had been sold.

It hadn't mentioned who had sold it, and when I had called the auction house to find out, they'd claimed they no longer had access to those records.

Considering we were at a distance of some decades from that sale, that was probably even true.

There had been no reports on the theft. The Elvyngs had kept that one very quiet. Why?

I heard the heavy *clunk* of one of the library's ancient brass doorknobs turning, and the door to the main reading-room swung open.

Jay stood upon the threshold, eyes wide.

'Hi,' I said, beaming.

Jay stared at me like I was some kind of apparition.

'What?' I said.

'How did I get here?'

'You... were expecting to end up somewhere else?'

Jay released the door, and composed himself. 'Actually, yes,' he said, ambling in. 'I've just left my room.'

So he'd expected to find the usual panelled passage-way beyond, and instead had been neatly whisked straight downstairs. 'House thinks you should visit us,' I suggested. 'I was thinking the same thing!'

It struck me that he was looking unusually smart. His beloved leather jacket was nowhere in sight; instead he wore a pair of neatly-pressed navy trousers and a matching jacket, with a white shirt underneath. Not a suit, but a far cry from jeans and leather.

'Been somewhere interesting?' I said, having looked him thoroughly up and down.

'Police station.'

'*What*?'

He grinned. 'I went voluntarily.'

'Jay, you're the last person I'd suspect of getting yourself arrested, ever. For any reason.'

'I can't decide whether you say that as a good thing.'

'I mean, I know I'm a rebel but I'm not *that* bad—'

'What did you get?' Val, impatient with our nonsense, firmly interrupted. Indeed, she directed her if-you-don't-*mind* look at Jay, the kind that sets new recruits all a-quiver.

Even Jay, a little, for he snapped to attention. 'Right. I wasn't getting anywhere trying to talk to them on the phone, so I went in person. Looking *respectable*.' For some reason, he appeared to be directing that last comment at me, for he frowned in my general direction. 'After some fast talking and a deal of flirting—'

'Flirting?' I blurted.

'Having taken a leaf or two out of the Book of Vesper—'

'*Me*? I'd never flirt my way into classified information.'

I got the raised eyebrows look from Jay *and* Val.

'Fine,' I sighed. 'Did it work?'

By way of answer, Jay pulled a notebook from a pocket and flipped through it. 'I did manage to blag my way into a look at the case file for the grimoire theft. I think. The Elvyngs weren't too open about which book it was or why it was important; the incident report listed it merely as "a valuable book", taken from the home of William Elvyng. Or, reported missing. Apparently there were no leads.'

'None? Not one?'

'No signs of forced entry, nothing else taken, no traces of any strangers in the house that day. I got the impression whoever responded to the call might have thought the Elvyngs were wasting their time.'

'You mean they might have made a false report of theft?'

'Which seems unlikely, before you get carried away with the idea,' Jay cautioned. 'Why would they do that? Insurance fraud? They have more money than they can spend already. It's more likely that, finding themselves stymied, the police were only too happy to declare it hokum and set the case aside.'

'And the Elvyngs let it go?' I stared. 'That's spectacularly unlikely.'

Jay restored the notebook to his pocket. 'They didn't chase the police about it, at any rate.'

'They hired a private detective,' I said. 'They must have.'

'You mean, besides us?'

'Definitely. It's been four years. We need to find out who that was, and whether they discovered anything.'

'Agreed.' Jay leaned against the nearest desk, hands in his pockets. 'What have you two dug up?'

'While you were charming paperwork out of the police? Not much,' I said. 'The theft wasn't picked up by the media, as there's no mention of it, and the book wasn't much talked about before, either. It seems to have been kept a deep, dark secret. And as far as I can tell, the Elvyngs have no enemies.'

Jay looked at Val.

'Don't look at me with the eyes of hope,' she said. 'So far I'm turning up nothing.'

'No four-year-old shady auctions purporting to be selling off the most remarkable spell-book in the world?'

'Not a one. Nor any chatter about thrilling heists pulled off against the most powerful magickal family in England.'

I gave a disappointed sigh, and laid my cheek upon my desk. 'Reality is so disheartening.'

'But there *was* a thrilling heist,' Jay said encouragingly. 'And it's the best kind.'

'The incredibly secret, no-one-could-possibly-track-us-down kind?'

'Exactly. Challenge accepted?'

I sat up again. 'Challenge accepted.' I withdrew my phone, and dialled the number I had wrung out of Crystobel. I hadn't yet had occasion to call her since she'd given us our unusual mission. I felt a curious flicker of anticipation — nerves? — upon doing so now.

She answered quickly. 'Miss Vesper?'

'Ves,' I said. 'Hi, Crystobel.' After the obligatory exchange of pleasantries, I said: 'Listen, we're going to need an invitation to your dad's house.'

'My father? Why?'

'We'd like a look at the place the grimoire used to be stored, and I'd really like to ask Mr. Elvyng a few questions about it.'

'I can arrange that,' she said.

'Great. Also, do you happen to know if anyone else was ever contracted to go after the grimoire?'

'Oh, yes. We went through three agencies at least. Father would have all the reports, I'm sure.'

'Three? And nobody found anything?'

'Nobody found enough, certainly.'

'I'm touched by your faith in us.'

'It's desperation, Miss Vesper. If the regular investigators have failed us, I am forced to look elsewhere.'

'So we're the wild card?'

'Something like that, yes.'

2

WILLIAM ELVYNG LIVED LESS than fifteen miles from the city of York, which was the home of his emporium and his academy.

Naturally, he had an entire stately home all to himself.

'Don't ask about his wife,' I said, as Jay and I drove up the driveway towards the house. The damned thing was huge — not so enormous as our House, of course, but crazily oversized for just one man. He had one of those elegant eighteenth-century piles, with a gorgeous symmetrical façade, formal gardens, stucco, a lake; everything.

'Why not?'

'She died, eleven years ago. According to the papers, William Elvyng never recovered.'

'Do you know everything about these people?'

'If I didn't before, I do now.'

Jay, still in his not-quite-a-suit, looked sharp. He'd done something to his hair, too, some kind of windswept-but-orderly style that rather suited him.

I felt a moment's envy; not over William Elvyng and his wonderful house, but the fortunate few towards whom Jay had directed his charm earlier in the day. I'd never seen him so well turned out.

I pulled up and parked just outside the handsome columned portico. I kid you not; as I got out of the car and smoothed my cream cotton dress, an actual butler appeared at the door to welcome us.

He even bowed. 'Miss Vesper and Mr. Patel?' he said.

'That's us.' I walked over, smilingly intent upon not turning my heel on the gravel driveway. The Elvyngs' butler was on the younger side, fortyish perhaps, with elegantly greying hair immaculately arranged, and a perfect dark suit, not too expensive.

'Is that William?' hissed Jay in my ear.

I shook my head. I'd seen pictures enough of Crystobel's father, and this wasn't him. 'Butler, I think,' I breathed.

Jay gave a tiny, almost inaudible snort.

Well, indeed.

I liked Mr. Butler, though, however incongruous his existence seemed in this day and age. He ushered us into the house as though we were honoured guests arriving for a garden party, and immediately promised to bring refreshments to the drawing-room. 'Mr. Elvyng is expecting you,' he said, and conducted us thither at once. He discreetly withdrew as soon as we were fairly through the door, presumably to fetch the aforementioned refreshments.

The interior of the manor matched its beautiful exterior, of course, in that it was perfectly maintained, and sumptuously decorated. The Elvyngs hadn't made a museum of the place, and filled it exclusively with period-appropriate antiques. Instead, they'd had a top-notch interior designer in. That fortunate soul had created a look obviously inspired by fashionable décor of the seventeen-hundreds, but with a modern update. The house was plush, luxurious and gorgeously coloured and I entered William Elvyng's drawing-room with a strong feeling that I could really make myself at home in his house.

My questing eye also detected more than one magickal trinket of interest and (no doubt) high value, artfully poised upon shelves and console tables. How the other half live, right?

William Elvyng was ensconced in an elegant, brocade armchair near the fire when we came in (an actual fire, despite the late summer heat beyond the walls of the manor). He rose upon seeing us, and came forward with outstretched hand and affable expressions of welcome. I admit to being agreeably surprised, though I don't know why. Had I expected a repellent personality to go with all this wealth and ease?

'So good of you to lend us your skills,' said Mr. Elvyng. 'Crystobel and I have always felt the greatest respect for the Society's work.'

Crystobel's father had an air of frailty about him, which perhaps explained the fire. He was rather older than I'd expected, considering Crystobel was only a few years off my own age. His pictures in the media I now realised were inaccurate, on the flattering side; he was well into his seventies and not in good health. His paper-white face, softened as it was with smiles, still had a pinched look about it, and his shoulders stooped. Someone had carefully arranged his thinning white hair to disguise an encroaching baldness.

'It's our pleasure,' I was saying smoothly, and with perfect truth. Everything about the mission appealed to me, from the sleuthing to the visiting notable people in their spectacular houses. Did I have a taste for splendour? Apparently. Was that somewhat inconvenient considering my profession and prospects? Rather.

I resolutely turned my eyes away from a beautiful gilded clock enthroned upon the mantel, and fixed them instead upon Mr. Elvyng.

'Is it all right if we ask you some questions about the grimoire?' Jay said. 'And the theft?'

'Certainly, certainly,' said Mr. Elvyng, gesturing us to take seats. He restored himself to the embrace of his own armchair with some care, and sat there looking as though a crane might be required to haul him out of it again. I felt rather touched that he had gone to the trouble of rising to greet us at all.

I installed myself upon the matched brocade sofa, conscious of a desire to move with an elegance to match the house, and folded my hands primly in my lap. 'The police reports were lacking,' I began. 'Can you tell us what happened on the day of the theft?'

Mr. Elvyng's lips twisted at my mention of the police. Clearly they had fallen some way short of impressing him. 'The problem was, Crystobel gave them too much information,' he said.

'Too much?' I repeated.

He nodded. 'She should never have mentioned Merlin's name. The officer who came to the house, well, he visibly stopped listening from that moment. Thought it some kind of publicity stunt, I believe. As though we need any more of that.'

I made a sympathetic noise.

'I kept the grimoire here, under my eye,' Mr. Elvyng continued. 'Perhaps that was foolish of me, but you understand — an irreplaceable item — I couldn't entrust it to one of the public buildings, with people going in and out all the time. And I couldn't be comfortable with it lying in a vault somewhere, either. I wanted it where I could personally see to its safety.

'Well, perhaps I could have prevented its theft — had I been here. But once or twice every year I pay an official visit to the Academy in York. It's expected. I go there to talk to the teachers, meet a few of the students, permit my photograph to be taken. That kind of thing. That year, when I returned, the grimoire was gone.'

'How soon did you discover it missing?' I said.

'Within a day or two of my return. It is — was — my regular habit to go into the room where it was kept, and look at it. Read a few pages. You understand, perhaps.'

'Absolutely,' I murmured, and I did. If I owned something that spectacular, I'd have a hard time leaving it alone.

So would Val.

'Well, I did so, perhaps, the day after I arrived home, and that's when I knew it was gone.'

'Where was it kept?' said Jay.

'You will be shown, shortly,' said Mr. Elvyng. 'But I kept it in its own annex off the library here at the house. The room has no access to the outdoors, and only one, small window, which is kept secure. I had a glass case created for it. It had every charm we could muster between us for its security, as I'm sure you can imagine. The thing is unbreakable, and kept locked at all times.'

'Was it broken?' said Jay.

Mr. Elvyng shook his head. 'Perfectly intact. The lock as well.'

'So someone had a key.'

'It appears so. Before you ask, there are two known keys in existence: one in my possession, and one in my daughter's. Both keys were accounted for at the time. Mine was with me at the Academy — I always carry it about with me — and Crystobel was travelling in France that week, her key with her.'

'So either someone managed to make a copy,' I mused, 'or the lock was opened by some other method.'

'Magickal, do you mean?' said Mr. Elvyng. 'It is not impossible, but nearly so. Believe me when I say the charms laid upon the case, lock included, were immensely powerful.'

I had no trouble believing him on that point. 'Was the lock made from argent, by any chance?' I asked, struck by a sudden insight.

His smile was faint. 'Very insightful, Ms. Vesper. The lock itself is made from commoner materials, but some of the mechanisms were worked from argent.'

'The keys, as well?'

Mr. Elvyng nodded.

The argent workings would be amplifying the effects of any charms laid upon them, which meant that the lock behind which Merlin's Grimoire had been kept was probably the most secure in the whole of England, if not beyond.

Interesting.

'Is there any way those charms could have been changed?' Jay said.

'If they were, they were changed back again before I discovered the theft,' said Mr. Elvyng. 'I noticed nothing amiss with the case.'

I wondered if the thoughts wandering through my own mind reflected Jay's at all. If Mr. Elvyng was right, and the case was so impregnable, what did that suggest? Either someone had managed to copy one of the two known keys without their owners knowing it, and that would be difficult indeed, if both of them were made from pure argent. Who but the Elvyngs have a supply of magickal silver lying about?

The alternative must be that the case showed no signs of being broken into because it hadn't been. Could it be possible that the apparent suspicions of the police had some truth to them after all? By Mr. Elvyng's account, the only people who could so neatly have made off with the grimoire were either himself or his daughter. If this was the tale they had told to the police, no wonder they hadn't been taken seriously.

3

'I SEE WHAT YOU are thinking,' said Mr. Elvyng, looking at me. 'I realise what the obvious solution must appear to be. But I beg you to believe it impossible. What motive might either I or my daughter have, for faking the theft of our own grimoire?'

A good question. I wanted to ask about insurance money; Crystobel had mentioned that there had been an insurance valuation made of the grimoire, which suggested a policy also. But the Elvyngs were rolling in wealth. Everything about them proclaimed as much. Why go to such lengths for even more?

'We made no claim upon the insurance policy,' continued Mr. Elvyng, and I began to feel unnerved. Were my thoughts written so clearly upon my face? Or was he actually reading my mind?

'Thank you for clearing that up,' I said crisply. 'One has to consider all the possibilities, of course.'

'Of course.'

All right, so if they hadn't even tried to claim the insurance then it wasn't a scam. But why hadn't they? Purely because it might look suspicious?

Well, they had no need of the money, and obviously hadn't purchased the grimoire as an investment. But then why have an insurance policy at all?

'Mr. Elvyng,' said Jay. 'Do you have any idea who might have taken the grimoire? Was there anyone who had shown signs of excessive interest in it, or who might have a grudge against your family?'

Mr. Elvyng was shaking his head. 'You must understand, a family in our position will always have its detractors. There are those who envy our prosperity, or who disagree with our values, and who are quick to say so. But I am not aware of anyone with any serious grudge. As for interest in the grimoire... again, such an acquisition must attract interest, but we have never widely publicised our possession of it. I doubt that many people even knew that we had it.'

'And what about within your own household?' I said. 'Who had access to this house four years ago?'

Mr. Elvyng gave a sigh. 'Yes, I understand the direction of your thoughts. I have had the same ideas, but I have of necessity dismissed them.'

Charming naivety, or just wishful thinking? 'I believe it must be considered our first line of investigation,' I said gently. 'Someone knew when you and your daughter would be away from home. Someone has managed to get past the charms placed upon the case, arguing a familiarity with the enchantments. And someone has got hold of a key, either one of the original two or an excellent copy. It *must* have been someone who had access to you or your daughter — more likely both of you — and opportunity enough to purloin your keys.'

'Perhaps also someone who could move about this house without exciting comment,' added Jay. 'Someone whose presence here would not be questioned. No one broke in, did they?'

'The police found no signs of forced entry,' agreed Mr. Elvyng. He looked diminished suddenly; tired? Or weighed down with regret?

'Who *was* here four years ago?' I prompted. 'Had they been with you for very long?' I had a feeling Mr. Elvyng had a good idea who might have taken the grimoire, and he didn't like it.

'I cannot fault your logic, Ms. Vesper,' said he. 'The problem is, there *was* no one else with access to this house, four years ago.'

My mouth opened in surprise. I had not seen *that* coming. 'No one?' I echoed dumbly. 'But what about that nice butler who admitted us?'

'My health has deteriorated in the past two years, enough that Crystobel has persuaded me to add to my staff here. Mr. Baker and his associates save me a deal of effort and they are trusted employees, but they are all of recent hire. I had no need of such, four years ago.'

'Cleaners?' said Jay. 'Gardeners?'

Mr. Elvyng's faint, crooked smile appeared again. 'Accomplished by magickal means, Mr. Patel. Then, and now.'

The Elvyngs had so much magick to throw around as to keep this entire manor — and its grounds — in perfect order without a single human employee? Giddy gods. What a glittering magickal heritage and a supply of raw argent couldn't do.

I cleared my throat. 'Er — and what about friends? Family members?' I hesitated to ask the question; no one wanted to consider that their nearest and dearest might have betrayed them.

'I have a sister,' said Mr. Elvyng. 'Her name is Anna Mason. She lives in America with her husband and children, and does not often come back. At the time of the theft, neither she nor her family had been near this house for at least a year.'

'Forgive me,' I said, 'but you are certain of that?'

'Yes. We have hired other investigators in the past few years. One of them conducted an exhaustive investigation into every connection of ours, and their traceable movements at the time. Anna was at home in Washington, together with Crystobel's uncle and cousins. My own cousin — Jessica — was in London. None of my friends or Crystobel's — few enough as they are — were seen anywhere near here that week, and I believe alibis were established for them all. So you see, it proved a fruitless line of enquiry.'

I exchanged a look of consternation with Jay. Everything Mr. Elvyng had said suggested a culprit known to the family, intimate with them; and yet, by this account, that was impossible.

What next, then? Could it really be the case that someone totally unconnected with the Elvyngs had pulled off such a seamless crime?

If so, we were dealing with — as Val had put it — a considerable power.

Mr. Elvyng did not conduct us himself to the grimoire's annex. Considering his obvious ill health, I had not expected it of him. It was the butler (or whatever he was), Mr. Baker, who extracted us from William Elvyng's fireside, and took us to the library. We left the Elvyng patriarch with a great many thanks (on both sides), and an invitation (from him) to call anytime we found ourselves with further questions.

The library at William Elvyng's manor was (dare I say it) slightly disappointing. I suppose I had got carried away with my imaginings, considering the illustrious nature of the erstwhile star of the Elvyngs' book collection. I'd expected a library to rival that of the Society. Instead, we were conducted into a handsome enough room, with a full complement of mahogany bookshelves, glass cases, polished desks and silken reading-chairs, but the actual quantity of books was rather modest. Probably they kept a great deal of their collection at the Academy, either for the daily use of the students, or in that cellar repository Jay had once talked of. These were just Mr. Elvyng's own books.

I took note of the environs as we walked among those immaculate shelves. Only one door lead into the room, and that opened onto a panelled corridor connecting the library to the drawing-room and whatever lay beyond. We were on the first floor, one level removed from the ground; I made a note to ask, later, about the staircases.

A second door occupied space on the far wall, but that led into the grimoire's annex. There was, as Mr. Elvyng had said, no other door there; certainly no way to get straight into that room from the outside. Whoever had taken the grimoire must have gone through a few other rooms at least, in order to reach this one. But then, I'd been working on the assumption that there must have been someone else in this sprawling pile of a manor at the time of the theft, even if Mr. Elvyng was away. But if that wasn't true, the thief had enjoyed the luxury of waltzing through an empty house on their way to steal the grimoire; there hadn't been anyone here to challenge them. All they had to do, then, was get in and out, without leaving any obvious signs that they had done so. Once inside, they would have had totally free rein.

Which made it strange that they hadn't taken the opportunity to empty the house of valuables while they had been inside. But the police report had clearly stated that nothing else was reported missing.

The annex proved to be tiny. It had space enough only for the sizeable glass case, set upon a sturdy and ornate carved-oak pedestal, within which the grimoire had once been housed. Besides that, there was nothing; only polished wood panelling and the window Mr. Elvyng had mentioned, which I saw at once was too small for anyone to fit through, unless they had done so by magickal means. But again, why would anybody need to do that, if the house was empty? They could come through one of the doors, and wander up the stairs at their leisure. Provided they managed to switch off or disable the house alarms, which such a manor would certainly have.

Jay, having prowled optimistically around the compact annex as though he might trip over something noteworthy, leaned over the grimoire's case until his nose almost touched the glass. 'Was all this built just for the grimoire, Mr. Baker?' he said. 'That you know of?'

'I'm afraid I couldn't say,' said Mr. Baker, who had taken up a discreet post just inside the door, and stood waiting with hands folded. 'It was before my time.'

Jay nodded. Whatever he was doing with his face two inches from the glass, I hoped he was uncovering something useful about the charms upon it.

'This must have been,' I said, patting the corner of the great glass box. 'It looks sized for a specific book.' There was an indentation in the velvet-covered interior, a perfect little nook in which a certain priceless grimoire could nestle. 'Maybe the whole annex, too. It has the appearance of a converted airing cupboard.'

'I was thinking the same thing,' said Jay. 'I wonder who built it?'

'And when? Was it done around the same time the grimoire was purchased, or more recently?'

Whoever had constructed the annex might never have known what it was intended to house. But then again, they might have — or made some guesses about it, later. Or perhaps whoever had stolen the grimoire had been able to consult with the builders, and gained some information from them, as to the location and security of the room. I made a note to enquire with Mr. Elvyng shortly as to the date of the annex's construction. If it had been thirty years ago, perhaps it was of no relevance now.

Jay and I left William Elvyng's manor feeling discouraged.

'I can see why multiple unnamed investigators abandoned the case,' I said despondently as we got into my car. 'There are no leads here at all.'

Jay shook his head, and sat staring sightlessly through the glass as I backed up and turned around.

'You didn't detect anything interesting about the glass case?' I prompted.

'Nothing. Whatever charms used to be on it are long gone.'

I sighed. 'So someone outside the Elvyngs' circle somehow managed to get into the house, past the alarms, and through the impenetrable enchantments on the glass case, which they somehow unlocked; proceeded to extract the grimoire, and then left again without leaving any trace behind?'

Jay said, 'Apparently.'

'Fingerprints?' It was a faint hope.

Swiftly dashed. 'Police report says no.'

'Footprints?'

'Nothing.'

'Jay. We're actually going to fail at this, aren't we?'

'No.'

'The police and three different investigators came up with nothing. What have we got that's going to make us different?'

Jay began ticking things off on his fingers. 'The finest, if untried, magickal sleuth in England, and her improbably musical sidekick.'

My eyebrows went up. 'That's us?'

'Resources of an unusual nature, presided over by the best librarian and book-sleuth in England.'

'Val and the magickal dark web.' I nodded. Fair.

'Breathtakingly high stakes.'

'You mean the inevitable and total decline of magick in all of Britain if we don't find Crystobel's crummy grimoire?'

'Motivating, no?'

I muttered something incomprehensible, even to me.

'Exactly when did it go from the most exciting book in the world to a "crummy grimoire", by the way?' said Jay.

'About halfway through our fruitless meeting with the obliging William Elvyng.'

'I wouldn't say it was fruitless. We have discovered several ways *not* to investigate this crime.'

'That would be more helpful if either of us could think of a single way *to* investigate this crime.'

'You're the great detective,' said Jay, tapping out some unrecognisable melody on the dashboard of my car. 'You can do this.'

'You believe in me.'

'I do.'

'Thanks.'

'Anytime.'

4

I MENTALLY BANGED MY face against the steering wheel. Expressions of implicit and unshakeable confidence are a lot nicer when you've got *something* to work with. Otherwise, it's the high road to disappointing your friends.

'What would Nancy Drew do,' I muttered.

Jay shook his head. 'No good. Being fictional, Nancy Drew always had a convenient lead.'

'How do you know?'

'I may have read some of them.'

'Uh huh?'

'Or a lot of them.'

I grinned. 'I knew there was a reason why I liked you.'

'Hopefully there are one or two more.'

'We can discuss that some other time.'

'I look forward to it.'

'All right, what would Poirot do? He didn't need leads. He just needed to think.'

Jay made a show of consulting the watch he didn't wear. 'Right. Some people work best under pressure, so I'm giving you five minutes to think.'

'Five?!'

'You've already wasted three seconds.'

I gulped. 'Thinking.'

And I did. For real.

'Time's up,' said Jay, what seemed like thirty seconds later. 'What have you got?'

'Motive.'

'More specifically?'

'Why would somebody steal this particular grimoire?'

'For one thing, it's incredibly valuable.'

'That's one possible reason. In which case, we're looking for a way someone might manage to sell a unique, priceless and recognisable grimoire for a fabulous sum without attracting notice.'

'For another thing, it's famous.'

'Right. It might be because of its purported author, in which case we're looking for someone with a Merlin obsession strong enough to consider it worth the manifold obstacles and risks involved with stealing it. I didn't think to ask Mr. Elvyng if anyone had ever offered to buy the book from him. I'll do that.'

'There's also hatred of the Elvyngs as a possible motive,' said Jay. 'So, spite.'

'I think we covered that one, though. If there's anyone out there with that level of a grudge against the family, they've been so quiet about it that we've no idea where to look for them.'

Jay nodded. 'Last option is the contents. Is there a charm in there someone would just about kill to get their hands on?'

'Possible, but tricky. For one thing, nothing either of the Elvyngs have said suggests they publicised the contents at all; indeed, they've had the strongest of motives not to. So who could even know what was in it?'

'They didn't always own it. Who had it thirty years ago?'

'Possible line of enquiry, but low priority. Thirty years is a *long* time. Why wait so long to steal it? Anyway, if it's someone who was familiar with it thirty years ago, they know the contents already. Why would they need the grimoire now?'

'So you're thinking it's most likely either the money or the cachet.'

'Yes. It's time to go consult with our favourite book-sleuth. I want to know about any known fences of rare and illegal spell-books.'

'You think Val would know?' Jay sounded shocked. Adorably so.

'Picture this. A woman — indeed, a Society — absolutely dedicated to rescuing beleaguered magickal paraphernalia wherever it may be found. And a world full of people eager to get their sticky hands on valuable artefacts, by means legal or otherwise. How many irreplaceable tomes end up changing hands on the black market, do you think? And how many would end up disappearing forever into the dubious care of unsuitable people, if somebody didn't intercept them?'

'Giddy gods,' said Jay. 'Val's a library superhero.'

'You should definitely tell her that.'

'No. She'll raise her brows at me.'

'You're scared of Val?'

'No!' said Jay, and coughed. 'Er. Aren't you?'

'Not in the least.'

'I knew you for a brave woman, but that beats everything.'

I didn't kick him, because I was driving, but he had a narrow escape.

Upon sharing my flashes of brilliance with Val, I found myself regarded — keenly — in a fashion I might term "surprised and impressed in equal measure".

'That's actually a great idea,' said she, patently astounded. What, was it so unlikely I'd come up with a good idea?

I swallowed my sense of injury. 'About the fence?'

If there was an eye-roll going on in response, I opted not to notice it. 'No. What do you think I've been scouring the dark web *for*, all this time? I've got an appointment set up for you already. Best fence in the business. Been working in the industry for twenty years.'

I chose not to contest Val's terming of black-market book trade as an "industry". 'And you just... made an appointment?'

'She's a friend.'

'Of course.'

Val closed the heavy old book she'd had spread open on her desk when we came in. 'No, I meant about the collectors. Lots of treasures vanish into private collections, and they don't always go through a fence, either. An occasional enterprising soul has been known to hire people especially for the purpose of acquiring some special piece, with or without the consent of a given artefact's present owner. And Merlin's just the type to attract that kind of crazy.'

'Question is,' I mused, 'if I were Merlin-obsessed and determined to possess his personal grimoire — or something said to be so — well, I can imagine I might be able to trace the sale of said grimoire into the Elvyngs' possession a few decades back. And I might guess that they wouldn't part with it again, not for mere cash. Supposing I'd resigned myself to a more questionable transfer of ownership, then, how would I go about hiring a team to steal it?'

'And without bringing the police straight down on my head,' added Jay.

'I'm not aware of a convenient yet somehow top-secret forum for thief hire, if that's what you're driving at,' said Val.

'I actually mean it literally. I'm not speculating. I want practical advice.'

'Ves?' said Jay. 'Don't say it.'

I said it. 'Forget scouring four-year-old records for traces of a spectacular book heist no one seems to know anything about. I want to hire a thief.'

Val stared at me. 'To steal what?'

'Something rare and Merlin-related, obviously.'

'Ves. From *where*?' That was Jay again, not quite expressing such deep-seated confidence in me as he had earlier.

'From here. Obviously.'

'Obviously.'

'I don't know if you knew, but we happen to have a priceless piece of Merlin memorabilia right here at the Society.'

'We do?' A flat stare from Val.

I nodded enthusiastically. 'His very own Wand, made from ancient amber and bone—'

'Yes. We have no such thing.'

'As far as the world is shortly going to be concerned, we do. It's in Ornelle's care and we've done our best to keep it a secret all this time because obviously it's precious, but some thoughtless person with a blabbing mouth will set all our care at nought, and broadcast its existence far and wide.'

Jay's face had gone into his long-suffering look.

'And whenever someone investigates they'll find a neat trail all over the magickal web pertaining to just such a Wand, indubitably the property of Merlin.'

'They will?' said Val. 'How's that to come about?'

'I'm sure you'll find a way.' I smiled seraphically.

Val's eyes narrowed. 'Then what?'

'Then I pose as a Merlin-crazed collector of near inexhaustible means, whose attempts to purchase the Wand have been brutally rebuffed. That greedy Society has to pay. They've no right to keep Merlin's Wand for themselves. It will serve them right to lose it!'

Silence.

'What?' I said. 'Jay! I asked you how we were going to be different from all those failed investigators. This is how.'

'By getting yourself arrested for instigating a robbery?'

'That won't happen.'

'*How not?*'

'Because we'll be careful.'

'We?'

'Come on! How can I be expected to pull this off without the help of my improbably musical sidekick?'

'You know you're not exactly popular with Ornelle already, right?'

'Right. She hates me anyway, nothing to lose.'

'There's still one problem here,' said Jay.

'Just the one?' said Val.

'How are we going to hire this legendary and as-yet unidentified thief team?'

'I'm guessing... word of mouth,' I said.

'What?'

'Rumour! No one just hangs out an ad for grand larceny—'

'You think?'

'—but if we were to let it be known, quietly, in certain circles, that we're in the market, word might get around.'

'*Which* certain circles?'

Poor Jay. I did exasperate him so. 'We do have an appointment with a notable fence?'

'Two *Society employees* have an appointment with a notable fence.'

'Not quite true,' said Val. 'I only told Sally I'd be sending a friend over. I didn't say what friend, or why.'

For all his supposed wariness of Val, Jay didn't pull any punches when he saw a problem. 'Do you think she's likely to believe you'd collude with said friend to commit a robbery against your own employer?'

'Why not?' said Val. 'People with shaky morals rarely have any difficulty believing in other people's.'

'So many years stuck at your desk,' I said. 'Slaving away for the Society. Long hours, low pay. You *deserve* the handsome fee you're going to get for helping me get hold of this Wand.'

Val smiled. 'Right. And the prospect of a job with inside help might be quite attractive to a professional thief, no?'

'Oh?' said Jay. 'Why aren't you just stealing the thing yourself, then, and selling it directly to the-collector-who-most-certainly-isn't-Ves-in-disguise?'

'First-time thief,' said Val promptly. 'I have qualms. Also mobility issues. No daring getaway in the nick of time for *me.*'

'She's sold you on this idea, hasn't she?'

'There was one true thing Ves said in all this nonsense. I *do* spend a god-awful amount of time at my desk. Wouldn't you fancy a change?'

Jay groaned. 'You're both getting arrested.'

'Ye of little faith,' said I. 'If you'll excuse me, I have an identity to prep.'

'I realise I'm making myself Mr. Unpopular here,' said Jay. 'Again. But you're overcomplicating this.'

'Please don't rain on my parade,' I said.

'If you want a parade, throw a birthday party,' Jay said brutally. 'This is an important mission for the future of magick.'

'And you've a better idea?' I said.

'Actually, I do.'

'Oh.'

'We aren't looking for whoever *extracted* the grimoire, are we? We're looking for whoever ended up with it afterwards.'

'What if they're the same person?' I said.

'They might be. Might not. Point is, we aren't actually the police. We're here to retrieve the grimoire, not to punish the burglars. There has to be an easier way to cut straight to whoever *has the grimoire now,* not whoever took it out of William Elvyng's house four years ago.'

'And that way is what?'

'If I might borrow the clever part of your plan—'

'Jay.' I gave him a wounded look. '*All* of it was clever.'

Jay ignored that. 'Hold an auction.'

'I'm not following.'

'A Wand has recently come to light, purported to have belonged to Merlin himself. It's in the hands of a private citizen at this time, and said (anonymous) person would like to flog it for the highest possible return. Supposing we establish convincing credentials for the thing, that ought to bring the collectors out in force, no? And nobody runs the risk of arrest.'

I felt a little deflated. It *was* a much better plan. 'Can I still dress up?'

'As whom?'

'I could be the private citizen flogging the shiny thing.'

'Which part of "anonymous" isn't getting through?'

I sighed. 'Party pooper.'

'I do foresee a problem,' said Val. 'We don't actually have a Wand that once belonged to Merlin. Forgive me if I'm wrong, but there are probably a few laws regarding deliberate fraud?'

'We aren't going to sell anything,' said Jay. 'We could have a kind of silent auction. Let people register to bid, and then at the last minute cancel it.'

'Cancel it why?'

'Our anonymous seller has had a fit of capriciousness and changed her mind.'

'Still smells strongly of fraud.'

Jay stared both of us down. 'Two minutes ago you were happy to hire a team of *professional thieves* to steal an equally fake artefact. *Now* you complain about a little mis-direction?'

'We're disappointed about the grand larceny,' I said. 'It's only natural.'

Jay rolled his eyes. 'Right. If we're agreed, I'm going to talk to Indira about manufacturing a certain fake but convincing Wand of Merlin.'

Jay exited stage left without another word.

Val busied herself shuffling papers.

'I suppose he's right,' I said forlornly.

Val grunted. 'I liked our plan better.'

'Me too.'

5

I WAS LATER COMFORTED to recall that I still had an appointment with "the best fence in the industry." Hey, you never know how things are going to turn out. If Sally had fenced the stolen grimoire, or knew who had, we could have answers right away. We wouldn't need Jay's fake auction. I left for the meeting with high hopes.

And Sally turned out to be nothing like I expected.

I mean, really. You talk of a legendary dealer in stolen magickal artefacts, I picture somebody shady-looking, possibly rather greasy. Someone used to a life of skulking in the shadows, evading the law. Someone who in some way looks the part.

I arrived — alone — at the location Val gave me for the meeting, dressed in my best meeting-master-criminals ensemble. That being a dark-coloured dress, smart but not too smart, and power heels. I didn't bother changing the powder-blue colour of my hair. The best fence in the business had to have a strong stomach. She couldn't be easily perturbed by little things like eccentric hair choices.

Sally had agreed to meet me at a tiny coffee shop in a remote town I've agreed to leave nameless. Partly because it isn't far from Home, the location of which is not for public consumption; partly because it isn't far from Sally's base of operations either. The meeting was set for ten in the morning, and when I arrived, the shop was duly deserted. Only one other patron was in evidence when I walked in: a stout man parked in a far corner, laptop open, headphones on, a tall latte set at his elbow.

Probably not Sally, I decided, and sat down with my mocha on the other side of the room, right by the window. We were hurtling towards September, and the weather was beginning to reflect that: the morning was overcast and drizzling with rain, and I watched a procession of miserable-looking people in drenched t-shirts pass by.

Sally turned out to have one characteristic one might expect of a master criminal: stealth. Intent as I was upon the people out on the cobbled street, I still didn't notice anybody turn in at the door to the coffee shop, and make her way over to my table. I merely became aware, all of a sudden, that I was no longer alone.

I slowly turned my head.

My new table-mate was Yllanfalen. That shocked me more than it ought; after all, just because they're improbably beautiful doesn't mean they can't be morally compromised, does it? Sally was about my mother's age, at least in appearance, but not one iota less gorgeous for it. Her silver hair was upswept, and secured with jewelled combs; she wore the wrinkles around her mouth and eyes with superb grace; and the smile she directed at me might be called devastating.

I was intrigued to notice that she had totally eschewed the smart-but-not-too-smart look that I'd chosen, opting instead for a dazzling peacock-blue dress and the most stunning black velvet coat.

Okay, nothing about Sally suggested she had any interest in skulking. Far from trying to pass unnoticed, she positively invited attention.

'Sally?' I said, realising belatedly that I had no idea of her surname.

She inclined her head, and sipped delicately at the coffee I hadn't seen her purchase. Espresso. Strong, black and uncompromising.

'You are Valerie's friend?' she said, in one of those melodious Yllanfalen voices.

I tell you, these people make you feel like such a crow. I cleared my throat. 'That's me. Thank you for agreeing to meet with me.'

She nodded, subjecting me to a casual scrutiny that didn't fool me for a second. Her seemingly idle gaze swept over me and missed nothing. 'And how may I help you, Ms. Vesper?'

I tried not to glance theatrically around the coffee shop to check for anyone listening in, then stagily lower my voice to talk to my companion. Honestly, nothing says "we are up to no good" more obviously than that. But it *is* so hard to help it when you're up to your eyeballs in nefarious deeds.

Emulating her effortless poise instead, I said: 'We are attempting to track down an item that went missing four years ago. It's of some importance that it is retrieved.'

'And when you retrieve it?' she said. 'What then will you do?'

'We aren't particularly interested in how the, er, transferral of ownership was effected, or by whose hand,' I said, conscious that she might have friends and contacts to protect. 'The item must return into the possession of its original owner. That's all we want.'

'Are you the original owner?'

I shook my head.

'Then what is in it for you?' She looked me over again. 'You are not an investigator of crimes, I think?'

'I work with Valerie,' I said. 'I'm not usually for hire in such cases, this is true. But the owner of this missing thing made us an offer we couldn't refuse.'

There was a pause. I imagined her weighing up the option of pumping me for further information, which I very much hoped she wouldn't. I could not tell her about the argent; what might not such a person demand, if she understood its existence?

'The Society's goals are ever enigmatic,' she murmured, sipping coffee.

'Not really. We rescue endangered magickal things. If we have to bend a few rules to do it, we will.'

Something like amusement sparked in her limpid green eyes. 'And you have no such questions to put to me?'

'I could ask you why you agreed to this meeting,' I conceded. 'And I could express all manner of curiosity as to your business. But all I really want to know is: were you involved in finding a new home for a certain priceless grimoire, about four years ago?'

'Grimoires often come up,' she said, setting down her empty cup. 'Some more valuable than others. A priceless one, however? I take it you do not exaggerate.'

'Only a little. It *has* been sold in living memory, so someone has put a price on it.' When I named the price in question, her eyebrows lifted. Just a fraction.

'I know of only a few spell-books that could command such a price,' she said.

My curiosity fired up at once. A few? What were the others? *Where* were the others?

But I controlled myself. *Stick to the mission, Ves. Get the job done.* 'Have any of them changed hands in the last few years?'

'Not to my knowledge.'

My heart sank. 'Nothing linked to a rather famous chap known as Merlin?' I tried.

The eyebrows went up again. 'That one, was it?' She pursed her lips, an expression of — strangely — displeasure crossing her serene face. Then she said, very softly, 'I did not know it had been stolen.'

The fact that so major a theft had occurred outside of her range of influence evidently irritated her.

'Something like that would normally reach your ears, would it?' I said.

She inclined her head. 'So much so that—' She stopped, and after a pause, went on. 'You are certain that it was stolen, are you?'

'Its owners have asserted that it was.'

'No private sale? With these old families, there can be embarrassment about straitened circumstances. Perhaps they might rather term it stolen, than admit it was sold for cash?'

'You might be right,' I allowed, not choosing to go into the question of the Elvyngs' wealth. 'But if so, why would they contract us to find it again? Why not let it quietly be forgotten?' And they offered a truly princely reward, too. That the Elvyngs might be strapped for cash must be unthinkable.

Her brow contracted into a frown. She said nothing, appearing abstracted. I suppose she was questioning how such a spectacular theft could have been conducted without her ever hearing of it.

That she was genuinely nonplussed was beyond question. I'd completely stymied her.

'I have nothing to tell you,' she said abruptly. 'And that ought not be possible.'

I didn't know what to say, so I drained the dregs of my mocha and waited.

'I will make enquiries,' she decided. The dark frown hadn't lifted from her brow. 'If I hear of anything relevant to you, I shall inform Valerie.'

She gave me scant opportunity to respond to this, for in another moment she was gone, whisking out of the coffee shop with the straight-backed, bristling posture of a seriously displeased woman.

Did she imagine someone had been deliberately hiding things from her? I had no idea what her operation might be like.

Clearly, though, someone was in for a bad afternoon.

'Well,' I said aloud, and looked about me. The meeting hadn't gone as I was hoping, but perhaps it had not been a total loss either. If anybody could find out some titbit of information about that theft, it must be someone with connections like Sally's.

In the meantime, we had a pretend auction to launch.

'Indira,' I said late that evening. 'You're a genius. I hope your brother tells you that every day.'

Jay's insanely talented sister ducked her head, unable to hide her pleased smile, but unwilling to show it off either. 'Thank you,' she muttered.

Honestly, the girl is amazing. She must be twentyish, but seems much younger — partly due to that persistent shyness, and a tendency to try to be invisible. But young as she is (or looks), there's no end to her brilliancies. Someday she's going to be a magickal legend.

On this occasion, she had thrilled me by bringing our new "Merlin's Wand" to the first-floor common room, where Jay and I were holed up for the evening. There are two particularly excellent arm-chairs in there, positioned on either side of a long window. They're plushy and huge and one of them is *mine.* The other is Jay's. We often sit up there in the evenings, watching the sun sink over the verdant grounds at Home, and drinking more chocolate than is good for us.

Indira has obviously figured us out by now. I spotted her slip into the room, and thread her way unerringly through the various clusters of chairs and coffee-tables, some of them occupied, on her way to our corner. She hadn't even checked to make sure we were there before she headed our way.

'It's perfect,' Jay said, excellent big brother that he is. He had it in his hands as he spoke, and I swear *I* could believe that exquisite thing had once belonged to someone extra-ordinarily powerful. Amber and bone. Rich, deep gold, and aged ivory-white. She'd crafted these materials into a Wand of remarkable beauty: slender, tapering, coiled and embossed, mounted into a gold filigree handle. Magick radiated from it, together with a palpable sense of antiquity. How had she contrived that?

No wonder she'd been recruited straight into Orlando's secret lab.

'I want to keep it,' I said. 'Can I keep it?'

Jay rolled his eyes at me.

'Um, maybe after the auction's finished,' said Indira.

I sat up. 'Really. Really? I could?'

She blinked, alarmed. 'Um — maybe if Milady says...?'

Right. Milady's call. I sank back down again. 'Well, you've outdone yourself, and I applaud you. We shouldn't have too much trouble passing off this beauty as Merlin-ware.'

Jay snorted with laughter. 'Merlin-ware? Watch out for her, Indira. She'll have you crafting up an entire line of Merlin-themed paraphernalia in no time.'

'The Society's always in need of more funding,' I said. 'You can't tell me Indira-designed Merlin-ware wouldn't fly off the shelves.'

'Someone's been spending too much time in the Elvyng Emporium,' Jay muttered.

'I maintain that they're onto something with that place.'

Indira bent over our glass-topped coffee table, and made an imperious gesture in the direction of the velvet-lined box she'd brought the Wand in. Jay, to my fascination, obediently put the pretty thing back.

'You're taking it away?' I said. 'Already?'

'Valerie needs it,' she said. 'It's got to be photographed and filmed.'

Right, for the fake provenance records Val would be industriously spreading around online. 'Pics for the rumour mill!' I said. 'I love my job.'

Jay exchanged a look with Indira. I could not flatter myself that it was a look of shared admiration for me. 'I get results,' I said defensively.

'Are we forgetting that this particular mad plan was my concoction?' said Jay.

'You're right.' I picked up my empty chocolate cup and toasted Jay with it. 'Here's to my unholy influence rubbing off on you.'

Indira, surprisingly, grinned.

6

Two days later, the internet was teeming with references to the spectacular "new find". Val and I had concocted a whole story for it. It was found among boxes of junk in some deceased person's attic, if you didn't know, and came to light during the preparations for an estate sale. Some discerning soul recognised its unique qualities, sent it for further analysis, and here we are. One priceless artefact bursting forth upon an astonished world.

And if you think no one would believe such a tale, just consider how many times some old master has been dug up out of somebody's boxes of junk, having vanished out of all knowledge generations before. These things happen.

Also, people believe what they want to believe, and some people *really* want to believe in Merlin.

Hurrah for tech, too, for the photos of the Wand (only slightly touched up, ahem) made the thing look even more spectacular than it did in the flesh.

But we soon ran into a problem.

'We can't hold the auction online,' Val said.

'Why not? It's perfect. We remain totally anonymous, and we barely have to deal with anyone. We just collect the information, cancel it, and move on.'

Val, hunched over her laptop doing who-knew-what, looked up at me at that. 'Ves. You've encountered the internet before?'

'Yes...?'

'And you still think everyone's going to give us their real names and contact details?'

I blinked. 'Um?'

'I could call that charmingly naïve,' she muttered, returning to her screen. 'Were I feeling generous.'

I coughed. 'Surely there are obligations to do so, with a legal and above-board auction—'

'*Internet*,' said Val, thundering away at something on her keyboard. 'If we can remain anonymous, so can everyone else. And they will. Especially anybody shady enough to have already stolen one major artefact, and in case you'd forgotten that's exactly who we are hoping to find.'

'But—'

'Besides, any collector worth their salt will be suspicious of hoaxes *exactly like this one*. It's not like it hasn't been tried before, albeit with different goals. They'll want to see the Wand. Satisfy themselves that it's legitimate. Without that, the serious collectors aren't going to show up.'

'Isn't that a bigger problem?' I said, slightly appalled. 'I mean, they can't satisfy themselves as to its legitimacy when it... isn't.'

'I know, but Orlando's work is virtually perfect. If you didn't know it was a fake, tell me you wouldn't be convinced. Go on.'

'Well, I—'

'You would. Because it *is* an artefact of great power. That's its secret. The only things it isn't are antiquated and belonging to Merlin. Well, it will pass for the former because the materials they used are ancient, even if the craftsmanship is fresh. And as for the latter, if someone's got a way to prove beyond doubt that an item belonged to someone who lived many hundreds of years ago — if he ever lived at all — I'd love to hear about it.'

'It's actually Indira's work,' I said.

'No,' she said, looking sharply up. 'Surely not.'

'With Orlando's guidance, no doubt, but yes. She made it.'

Val looked at me for a long moment, then returned to her typing. 'We probably aren't paying her enough.'

'So we need to hold a real auction?' I said, backtracking a bit. 'In a real place?'

'Probably.'

'Isn't that risky? Won't the collectors be angry if they show up expecting to bid, and the auction's cancelled?'

'Ves complaining about risks,' Val muttered. 'That's a first.'

'I'm not *totally* devoid of a sense of responsibility.'

Val snorted.

'I'm surprised Jay hasn't been saying the same things,' I persevered.

'He might have, if it wasn't for the fact that our plan was far riskier. As the best of two risky options—'

'Did we announce yet that there's going to be an auction?'

'Not yet. That's tomorrow.'

'Okay. Why does it have to change hands?'

'Dear Ves, if you could please get around to making sense? I *am* rather busy this morning.'

'I might be about to override Jay's brilliant plan.'

'You mean the same way he overrode yours? Revenge is sweet.'

'Especially when it's also practical. Can't we just have an exhibition?'

'We...' Val sat, blinking. 'Actually, we could.'

'It gets better.' I admit to some feelings of smugness.

One eyebrow went up. 'Better? Or worse?'

'We're trying to lure a thief,' I said, letting that pass. 'How about we put it on display somewhere — strictly limited time, showing it off to the world before it vanishes into some private collection, etc — and then we put a tracker on it.'

Val said nothing.

'You know, like the ones we have on Jay's stuff.'

'I know what a tracker is.'

'Right. Well, anyone so desperate to own Merlin's grimoire as to steal it would probably want to make off with this, too. No?'

'Maybe.'

'And if they didn't just try to buy the grimoire — and they didn't, Mr. Elvyng said no one ever approached him with an offer — maybe that means they don't have that kind of money. In which case, an auction would be no good anyway.'

'You're just in love with the idea of master thieves pulling off spectacular artefact heists.'

'I... might be.'

'Mm. And what were the chances of your having become just such a thief, if the Society hadn't recruited you?'

'I believe you are casting aspersions upon my morals.'

'Grave ones.'

'I resent that.'

'So it isn't true?'

I thought it over. 'It would've been that or a great detective.'

'Two sides of the same coin.'

'So we're doing it?'

'What? The latest new and brilliant plan?'

'Exhibition! Come on!'

'I'm not sure I'm loving this pick-and-mix, trial-and-error approach to planning. Can we please stick with this one now?'

'We're going with it,' I promised.

'You still have to get it past Jay,' Val said.

'Right.'

'And Milady,' she added as an afterthought.

To my surprise, and secret satisfaction, Jay took the overthrow of his plan with grace.

Actually, more than that. Enthusiasm.

'That actually works far better,' he said. 'I couldn't quite work out how to handle the auction structure without making a mess.'

'It *was* a better plan than my other idea,' I allowed, generous in victory.

'Milady will be happier with it, too. She frowned a lot when I told her about mine.'

'Frowned? Jay, she's a disembodied voice.'

'I know, but sometimes you can hear the frown.'

'I'll tell her,' I promised.

'You do that. I'll go find an exhibition venue.'

'Not too close to Home,' I warned. 'We don't want anyone making any connection with us.'

'Right.' He stood up, and retrieved his jacket. 'I'd better tell Indira to build a tracker into the Wand. Sticking one on isn't going to cut it. Any thief worth their salt would be ready for that.'

'Good point.' I saluted.

'What's that for?'

'I'm saluting your practical turn of mind.'

'Literally saluting? I feel honoured.'

I bowed.

'Let's not overdo it.'

'Right.'

'IT IS A CLEVER scheme,' said Milady a little later, after I'd presented myself at the door of her tower-top room and awaited admittance. She'd been busy. I'd had to wait nearly half an hour. 'I trust all proper precautions will be taken?'

'Er, no doubt,' I said.

'Such as?' Milady prompted.

'Um, we'll hold the exhibition well away from Home.'

'Yes, that would be wise.'

'And...' I stopped, empty of ideas.

'Trust Indira's tracker, rather than lying in wait for the thieves ourselves?' said Milady.

I was silent with dismay.

'Ves?'

'How did you know?' I said in a small voice.

'I have known you for a considerable period.'

'And you still employ me!'

'I have great faith in your abilities, but that does not mean that I wish for you to needlessly endanger yourself in the pursuit of this grimoire.'

'Yes, ma'am.'

'Or Jay, or Valerie, or Indira either.'

'Yes, ma'am.' I almost saluted again, but thought better of it.

'Have you considered the probable consequences of failure?'

'You mean nobody steals the Wand?'

'That is one possibility.'

'If that doesn't happen, well, we'll still have attracted the notice of a lot of people who are interested in putative Merlin artefacts. We can investigate anyone who shows a particular preoccupation with it.'

'Good. What else?'

'Um.' I thought. 'If someone does steal it but the tracker doesn't work?'

'Also a possibility.'

'I have faith in Indira's craftsmanship.'

'So do I, but if we are dealing with an experienced thief — and we hope that we are — it is very possible they will be prepared for such things. It is not an unusual way of protecting artefacts of great value.'

'We'll have to be quick. Get after them the moment it's gone. All we need is a lead.'

'So you'll watch it day and night?'

'Yes...'

'And who among my Society is to be involved in apprehending these thieves?'

'Are we apprehending them? We only want to know where they take the Wand. Presumably it will be the same place they took the grimoire.'

'And if it isn't?'

'Um.'

'If, for example, the Wand is taken by someone else altogether, with no connection to the theft of the grimoire?'

I thought rapidly. 'That *could* happen, but it would be a huge coincidence. Too big, surely? How many obsessed Merlin collectors with inadequate moral fibre can there be?'

'There might be those whose interest is not in its provenance but in its value,' Milady pursued.

'Grab it and flog it? That's true.'

Milady relented. 'There have been no such thefts reported in some time, however, so I should think it unlikely.'

'Right!'

'It is a good scheme, Ves, but it is also a long shot. I hope you have other avenues of investigation in progress?'

'There's Sally.'

'Very well, tell me about Sally.'

I hesitated, struck by sudden doubt. Milady did *know* about Val's adventures in the bookish black market? What if she didn't, and took exception to Val's underworld connections?

But I banished the thought. Valerie would never try to deceive Milady upon such a point. Nor would she succeed. Milady, somehow, knew everything that happened at Home.

So I told her all about Sally, and her shock at such a theft's having occurred without her knowledge.

Milady seemed more interested in that fact than I had been. 'That is curious,' said she. 'It suggests, does it not, that perhaps we are not dealing with a team of career thieves? Surely those are precisely the kinds of people Sally would deal with. Or at least have some awareness of.'

'You mean maybe there was no heist?'

'Not as we have imagined it. I think perhaps a previous notion might prove correct: the thief and the new owner of the grimoire are the same person. Sally heard of no sale because there *was* no sale.'

'Then that person must be formidable indeed. The security at that manor is top-notch, and to get past the charms on the case — to take on the Elvyngs —' I remembered what Val had said, when we'd first entreated her help. *I rather fear we're dealing with a considerable power.*

'Going back to what I said about reasonable precautions,' said Milady.

'Yes. We'll be careful.'

'I shall send Rob with you.'

'Scary Rob. Yes, please.'

Our business complete, I bowed myself out and began my noisy clattering back down the stairs. I was halfway down when I felt a strong tug upon my heart. A strong, *urgent* tug, with a shade of panic to it.

Addie.

This new familiar-bond of ours had produced all kinds of effects I hadn't anticipated. I was in tune with Adeline's feelings and well-being in ways I had never been before; not all the time, but I received odd pulses of awareness at intervals, some of them rather strong.

I hadn't felt anything like this from her before.

Throwing dignity to the winds, I thundered down the rest of the stairs, and took off for Addie's glade at a dead run.

7

I DON'T RECOMMEND RUNNING that kind of distance in slip-on summer sandals. I had to take them off halfway to the glade, having almost tripped and brained myself on one of the ancient oaks marching along cither side of the driveway (those gnarly old roots are deadly). I arrived sweat-bathed, out of breath and with shredded feet.

Addie had acquired some new vegetation. Something frilly and pungently-scented met my senses as I entered the unicorn glade, its long, narrow leaves displaying an unusual array of colours. There were so many of these bushes, I couldn't even see the pool at the heart of the glade.

Or Addie either.

'Addie!' I yelled, with as much breath as I could muster. Everything was quiet. Too quiet. Nothing stirred at all, and not only was Addie herself nowhere in sight, but her — *our* — other friends were absent, too.

I stood frozen for one horrible moment, my heart pounding, visions of disaster spinning through my brain. Someone had discovered the glade. Someone had taken Addie and the others away.

A soft *whuffi* interrupted this sickening train of thought, and something shoved me from behind, hard enough almost to knock me over.

I recognised that *whuffi*.

I spun on my hooves, tail swishing, horn held high.

Addie planted her feet, lifted her head, and *whuffied*. Again.

'You have got to be kidding me,' I said, the words emerging as a series of *whuffis*. 'You're having a *chip emergency?* That's what you brought me running out here for?'

'*Whuffi*,' said Addie.

'A lack of chips is not an emergency, Addie! Giddy gods! You almost gave me a heart attack!'

'Whuff,' said Addie, with less defiance.

'And as you can see, I have brought zero chips. I expected to find you kidnapped or injured or dismembered or something, not *hungry*.'

Addie's head lowered, but she declined to reply, seeming intent upon chewing a long stalk of grass pressed between her lips.

'I mean, I'd get bored of eating grass too, I grant you. And I have been a bit preoccupied lately. I should have brought you a basin of chips days ago and I apologise.'

Addie whickered, and spat out the grass.

'Nonetheless, you can't panic-summon me every time you fancy some fast food. It isn't on and I won't have it. There's only so many heart attacks a girl can survive, you know?'

Addie gave me a flat stare, which I chose to interpret as semi-defiant capitulation. *Fine, have it your way.*

'Thank you,' I said, and looked around. Still no sign of the others. 'Where are the girls? You haven't eaten them in a fit of ravening hunger?'

A snort. Addie turned and, tail swishing, trotted away into the bushes.

I followed after.

Jay found me there sometime later. Probably some hours later, judging from the poorly-concealed exasperation I saw on him.

'Ves,' he said, picking me out from the line-up of unicorn ladies with unerring accuracy. I wonder sometimes what I look like. All I've seen of my own unicorn-form is the hazy, swishy reflection the pool can offer me, which is imprecise. I *think* I have a rainbow mane, but that might just be wishful thinking.

I dipped my head in acknowledgement of this salutation.

'Is there some reason why now seemed like a perfect time to take a horn holiday?'

Horn holiday. I laughed so hard I choked on my own nose-hair.

Jay watched me with widened eyes. 'Is that— are you dying? What's happening?'

I controlled myself. 'I'm fine,' I said. *Whuffi, whuffi.* 'Did you bring any chips?'

I knew the answer already: no. I'd have smelt them otherwise. So would Addie, and she'd be presently mowing Jay down in her haste to devour every greasy, delectable morsel.

'I didn't bring any pancakes,' Jay said, nearly but not quite interpreting me correctly. Not bad, huh? 'I wasn't expecting to need any,' he said, a little apologetically. 'But if you'll come back Home with me, we can probably persuade Kitchen to rectify that.'

'I *love* Kitchen!' I declared, and frisked over to Jay. Kitchen could probably be persuaded to rustle up a bucket of chips for Addie and the girls, too — better make it two or three buckets — and then maybe my beloved Familiar would leave me in peace for a little while, so we could get on with the important business of pulling off a daring hoax.

I fell into step beside Jay, and we made our way at a slow amble out of Addie's perfect, peaceful little glade.

The moment I stepped over the invisible threshold, my hooves and horn disappeared again, leaving me human-Ves.

'Horn holiday,' I said, giggling.

Jay carefully avoided looking at me. 'I should have thought to bring you a new dress, too. Honestly wasn't very organised today.'

'Oh! That's okay. I seem to have worked out how to hang onto my clothes.' I was indeed dressed in my summer silks once more, though my sandals had vanished, probably never to be seen again.

Jay shot me a startled look. 'How did you manage that?'

'No clue.'

'Nice one.'

A LITTLE LATER, ONE Ves (and one Jay) having been suitably stuffed with banana-split pancakes, and one herd of unicorns having been suitably plied with unhealthy snacks, Jay and I flopped into our usual flumping-spots in the common room and exchanged notes.

'So why exactly were you hobnobbing with the horn squad?' he said.

I tried to keep a straight face, really I did.

After ten seconds or so of solid giggling on my part, Jay lost his composure, and began to laugh as well. 'Sorry. I shouldn't do that when I want a straight answer out of you.'

I took a deep breath, only slightly wobbly in the middle, and managed to get a grip. 'Addie had an emergency. A real, honest-to-god, sirens-sounding, help-me-this-instant emergency. I almost broke my neck hurtling down the stairs from Milady's tower, and my poor feet may never recover from my mad dash out to the glade.' I displayed the ruined soles of my feet for Jay's inspection.

He made a sympathetic noise. 'And what was the emergency?'

'Lack of chips. Honestly, it's inspiring. Next time I have a pancake craving but no pancakes, I'm getting me an air-raid siren. *That* should fetch you all running.'

'I'll make a note,' Jay promised. 'If the air-raid sounds, it's straight down to the cellar, or risk being mauled to death by Hangry Ves.'

'Hangry? I am never hangry.'

'No, that's true. Really you just look forlorn and a bit pitiful, like a sad puppy.'

My dignity did not especially like that idea. I sniffed.

Jay grinned. 'It's okay. It's cute.'

Cute. Huh.

'Anyway,' I said. 'Why were you looking for me again?'

'Oh, because everything's ready. Project Hoax launches in the morning.'

'Project Hoax? Subtle much?'

'It's accurate. Does what it says on the tin.'

'Fair.'

Jay went down a list of details, proving that he and Val had thought of basically everything. I felt a twinge of compunction. Jay was right, I shouldn't have spent the whole day hobnobbing with the horn squad. I should have been helping Val and Jay. And Rob, who had an entire security, surveillance and pursuit plan mapped out and it was only seven o'clock in the evening.

I hadn't meant to spend the whole day in there, honest. It can be hard to keep track of time as a unicorn. I'd swear I had been there for only a couple of hours.

'So we should get an early night,' he finished, demonstrating once again what a responsible Boy Scout he is. 'You especially.'

'Why me especially?'

'Because you're hosting.'

'What?'

He grinned. 'We're keeping the identity of the supposed owner "anonymous". This exhibition is being handled by a professional events agency, the face of which is you.'

'Jay. A public exhibition, attracting everyone who's anyone in magick? People will recognise me. Even if I wear—' I paused to take a breath, shuddering '—*ordinary* hair.'

'I know. That's why we're putting you in disguise.'

My eyebrows rose.

'You did want to play dressing-up?'

'What, are you going to give me a new face?'

'No.'

'Of course not.'

'But we are giving you the appearance of a new face.'

I sucked in a breath. Advanced illusion work? That shit was expensive.

And incredibly fun.

'Who am I going to be?' I asked, breathless with anticipation.

'We thought we'd leave that up to you.'

I bounced in my seat.

'But!' Jay raised a warning hand. 'Don't go too crazy, okay? We want your persona to be believable.'

I crossed my heart. 'Soul of discretion,' I promised.

Jay's look was profoundly sceptical.

One thing it's difficult for illusion-work to do, however intricate, is give an inaccurate impression of height. If you haven't got the bulk, you haven't got it; it's no use trying to stick two extra feet of height onto yourself. I mean, what are you going to put in it? Thin air?

So I went for a form suited to my stunted stature.

'Spriggan?' said Jay, when I finally emerged from Home's hair-and-makeup team (so to speak).

I patted my hair. I hadn't gone for anything too nuts, as per Jay's request. They'd given me a blue rinse and a crown of braids, attractive but also professional.

Oh, and they'd aged me up by about sixty years.

'That's it?' I said. 'That's all you're going to comment on?'

Jay looked me over. 'Anything else I should consider noteworthy?'

'How about my transformation into a ninety-year-old woman?'

'I'm sure you had your reasons.'

'Respectability,' I informed him, though he hadn't precisely enquired. 'People trust kindly old ladies, don't they?'

'Are you going to be kindly?'

'With a bit of brisk efficiency thrown in. No doddering though.'

Jay nodded gravely. 'There can't be any doddering. The entire mission would be thrown into jeopardy.'

I squinted at him. 'My name, in case you're interested, is Cornelia Spink.'

His face didn't even twitch.

'Fine,' I sighed. 'Actually it's Cornelia Morgan.'

'Very well, Ms. Morgan,' said Jay. 'If you'll be so good as to come with me, we'll pop off to your waiting venue, maybe get you a nice cup of tea and a biscuit.'

'I hope that isn't an age joke,' I said severely.

'Not in the least.'

'I *like* a nice cup of tea and a biscuit, even when I'm not being ninety.'

'Even at the tender age of thirty-one?' Jay said, incredulous. 'Surely not.'

I thwapped him with my respectably taupe-coloured handbag. 'As, may I remind you, do you.'

Jay grinned, relenting. 'I was hoping for a nice cup of tea and a biscuit myself.'

'Will there be custard creams?'

'Absolutely without question.'

Off we popped.

8

JAY, PROBABLY WISELY, HAD eschewed pomp and gone for basic. He'd hired a low-key exhibition hall in a town so dull and unremarkable I can't even remember its name. Possibly some of these choices had come about due to lack of time and lack of resources (we couldn't exactly expect our clients — or the Society — to pay for the party of the century, after all). But it worked out well. We wanted people to show up for the Wand, not for the hors d'oeuvres. That should hopefully limit our visitor list to those with a sincere interest, either in magickal rarities or in Merlin paraphernalia. Hopefully both.

They didn't take me there in a limousine, either, slightly to my disappointment. Jay having declined to try to haul everybody there via the Ways, one by one, he had sensibly hired a bus instead. Or more accurately, a coach.

Took me straight back to my school days, I can tell you. I tried to behave like a responsible adult, and mostly succeeded — in that I spent half the journey eating sweets with noisy wrappers, but I resisted the temptation to screw up those wrappers and turf them at Jay's head. Or Rob's.

It's a mark of affection. Really.

Jay, unfazed, sat with headphones on the entire way, ignoring the lot of us. I asked him later what he'd been listening to.

'History podcast,' he said.

'Very educational.'

'I didn't want to waste the time,' said he earnestly.

This is why, in twenty years' time, the Patels will have taken over the world.

And I'll be a fifty-something unicorn, skulking in Addie's glade and wondering where it all went.

Anyway.

I'll spare you the details of arrival and set-up and so on. It's not very interesting. Much of it was done by the time we got there, anyway; we had a ready-to-use venue, with a gorgeous (and, thanks to Rob, very secure) enchanted-glass case waiting to receive our priceless Wand. Ornelle had insisted on conveying the Wand itself, patently distrusting the rest of us to keep it safe. Me, especially. She kept shooting me scowly-looks, despite my disguise, and wouldn't let me anywhere near the case until it was safely locked down.

I might have been offended, except for two things. One: I'm the only person in the country whose pet is a master treasure-thief in her own right (even if Pup has rather deserted me for Miranda, lately. Hmph). Two: there is the small matter of what became of the Sunstone Wand I wasn't supposed to have kept forever, and then went on to... permanently lose.

So I quietly kept myself away from the pretty glass case, until it was so securely secured I'd have to throw a house at it to get it open again.

(That last part might seem counter-productive, considering we were hoping someone would steal it. But think about it. You're a thief with some experience. You know exactly the level of security people tend to employ where priceless valuables are concerned. Then you show up with your thieving-suit on, all ready to burgle, and find the valuables in question in a case a toddler could break into. You'd pretty much smell a rat at that point, wouldn't you? So we went for ultra-secure).

Rob had brought a team of security personnel along with him. Kind of like a batch of mini Scary-Robs. They looked the part, with dark clothes and stern visages, and I had no doubt every one of them had one of the Society's most powerful Wands tucked away somewhere within easy reach. These were stationed near every exit, with two of them in the hall with the Wand. They were there for effect, as much as anything; they really made it look like we had something irreplaceable in there.

But they were also poised to protect the rest of us, in case our thief proved dangerous — and to launch the pursuit, as soon as our thief had (hopefully) got away with the Wand.

We had several other Society staff stationed about the hall, ready to talk glibly to our visitors about the Wand's manufactured but terribly fascinating history. Jay was one of these, looking sharp in a dark blue suit. He'd got a pass from Milady on that one, seeing as he was too new to the Society yet to be widely recognisable as one of ours.

And of course we had me, disguised up to the roots of my hair, and doing a great job of fluttering about checking things, fiddling with stuff and generally looking very pro-fessional and experienced.

When the doors opened on the dot of nine o'clock, we were ready.

Oh wait, except for one thing.

The priceless Wand lay in its case looking *really* great — once you got up close to it. From a distance, though, we had a boring glass case with nothing much in it and that wouldn't do. My sense of showmanship wasn't having it.

With a sneaky, surreptitious little bit of magick, I gave the Wand a glow. It's the same charm I use to throw out light-balls when I need to see where I'm going, except slightly modified.

When I had soft rainbow lights beaming gently from inside the enchanted glass case, I was satisfied, and could move away.

I definitely didn't notice Jay rolling his eyes at me from the other side of the room.

'What?' I mouthed, shrugging. Who doesn't love a bit of rainbow light with their ancient magickal artefacts?

I had to stop there, because people were coming in. Already. Two minutes after nine and there was a flood of them. An entire flood. They filled the hall inside of ten minutes, and we had to start a queuing system to allow people to view the Wand.

I watched this in stupefied silence for a minute or two, thinking back over all the things Val had done to get the word out about the Wand. I tell you, if that woman ever gets tired of being Goddess of Library, she'd be spectacular in public relations.

Then I snapped out of it, for as events co-ordinator it was my job to deal with this ocean of eager spectators. And so, with *zero* doddering, I got on with it.

I had two theories about how the theft might go down.

One option: it could happen at the busiest time of the day, when the staff were swamped and harassed and there were so many people milling around, no one would notice the thief. And I was prepared for that, all through the long hours that followed, for honestly the entire day was the busiest time of the day, and none of us had so much as a moment to breathe.

But the Wand remained in its glass case, untouched. And no wonder, really. Thinking about it in the abstract, it had seemed like a good time to steal an artefact, but when I was in the middle of it all I soon realised that was absurd. No thief, however clever, could get near the thing without the unwanted supervision of various staff, not to mention seventy-five impatient exhibition-goers eager for their turn.

So the other possibility had to be the other extreme: when the exhibition was at its quietest. First thing in the morning, I had thought, but that had turned out to be nonsense. There was no quiet period first thing that morning. So that left the very end of the day, when the flow of people had ebbed, and the staff were too exhausted and harried to keep quite the same watch on the Wand as we had been earlier in the day. That was when a sneak-thief might find it possible to slink in, do their thing, and slink out again with a certain treasure up their sleeve.

Unfortunately, by the end of the day, we *were* too exhausted to do a great job of keeping up our watch.

But that came later.

What happened first was a Distraction.

Not the spectacular kind that would draw the guards away from the Wand and give the thief an opportunity to steal it. Nothing so spectacular.

The distraction was of a personal nature, and only effective upon me, because at about half past two in the afternoon, Baron Alban walked in.

No. Prince Alban, Ves. *Prince.*

In he came, dressed in a pale summer suit with a fedora — an actual *fedora*, for goodness sake, and gods did it suit him — and spotted me at once.

Over he strolled, scarcely inconvenienced by the hordes of people in between him and me. It's the height, perhaps, and the air of confidence. People got out of his way.

And I, forgetting I was disguised as a ninety-year-old spriggan, promptly went smiley and blushy.

'It's been a while,' I said, beaming up at him.

'I know,' he said. 'I'm sorry. I've wanted to come by for ages, but my schedule…'

He didn't elaborate, but I remembered what had been keeping him so busy lately. My smiles went out like snuffed candles.

'I hope the tour went well?' I said, with tolerable composure. He'd been swanning about on the continent with his wife, sweet-talking his fellow European royals, and generally doing pretty fabulously at PR himself.

'As far as I could tell,' he said, smiling his handsome smile. 'You know how these things go. Everybody smiles and says the right things, and if they're secretly thinking something different you'd never know it.'

I nodded sympathetically. 'That must be difficult.' I blinked as my tangled thoughts lit upon a more pressing idea. 'Wait. How did you know I was here?' I felt a flutter of panic. What if word had leaked out about the Society's involvement with the Wand? What if everyone knew it was us?

'I didn't,' he said, and the hammering of my heart eased. A bit. 'I came to see Merlin's Wand.'

That didn't quite explain everything.

His response to my questioning look was a wide grin. 'I knew you the second I walked in here,' he said.

'What! But—' I looked down at myself, indignant. It was a *great* disguise. How could anybody possibly see through it?

He shrugged. 'I'd know you anywhere. You're too... *you*.'

I squinted up at him, unsure whether to take this as a compliment. 'You have the honour of addressing Ms.

Cornelia Morgan,' I informed him. 'I am the co-ordinator of this little event.'

'Pinnacle of your long career, no doubt?' His eyes were doing their twinkly thing, the one that melted my insides.

I nodded primly. 'And if you'll excuse me, I have work to do.' I didn't want to walk away, but on the other hand I really did. The Baron — *Prince* — wasn't the kind of distraction I could afford on that of all days.

He nodded. 'I can see that you're busy. What time do you close up?'

'Um. Around five? Hopefully.' If the seemingly endless flow of humanity — and other beings — had finally ebbed.

'Dinner?' He smiled.

And I hesitated. I wanted to say yes. I so badly wanted to say yes, but he was a prince and a married one, and a mere, foolish Ves had no business getting herself too mixed up with any of that.

And I caught Jay's eye. He was busily feeding people into and out of the viewing queue, but half his attention was fixed upon me and Alban, and while he was as composed as usual, I detected signs of concern in the dark looks he kept directing at me.

He met my eyes for a long moment, and while I couldn't read everything that was going on in his mind, it certainly was nothing good.

'I—' I began. Great, now I was stammering like a fool. 'Actually, I already have dinner plans,' I said, and I didn't have to feign regret.

Alban hadn't missed the direction of my gaze. 'With Jay?' he said, with a trace of surprise.

'Yes,' I said.

He nodded, and backed up so fast he almost squashed the old lady trying to pass behind him. 'Great,' he said heartily. 'Have fun! I'll catch up with you soon, all right?'

And he left, still smiling.

That damned *smile.* I looked ahead into the far future, and predicted miserably that I never would find it other than devastating.

I took a breath, tried unsuccessfully to calm the turbulent sensations discomposing my guts, and went back to my job.

9

'IN CASE YOU DIDN'T know,' I said to Jay later, 'we have dinner plans.'

He didn't say anything. He looked too pole-axed to form words.

'Is... that bad?' I said, and my heart did a little sinking thing. It hadn't occurred to me that Jay might dislike the idea. Or — what if he already had dinner plans with someone else?

'No,' he said, but too cautiously to make me feel much better. 'I thought you'd — you aren't doing something with Alban?'

'He did ask me,' I said. 'But seeing as I'd already made plans with you, I didn't feel that I could accept.'

Jay digested that. 'I am honoured to serve as your excuse,' he said, not looking at all honoured.

My heart sank a little bit more. 'We— we could reframe that,' I tried. 'How about my preference?'

'Am I?'

I thought, guiltily, of how much I'd wanted to accept Alban's invitation.

Then I thought about what dinner with him would actually be like. Me, blushy and smiley on the outside, sick at heart on the inside, trying not to be pathetically weak to all the Baron's charms and failing miserably.

Dinner with Jay, though? That would be fun. Just, fun. We'd talk, go over the events of the day. Make plans for tomorrow. Make each other laugh. And Jay would smile at me sometimes and all it would do to me was brighten my day.

No drama.

'Actually,' I said, 'you are.'

I was rewarded with a smile. It was only a tiny one, but it went all the way up to his eyes, so I'm counting it. 'Then it's a deal,' he said.

I beamed. 'Great. Till later, then.'

We sealed the deal with a fist-bump, and went back to herding people for another couple of hours.

As I might have slightly hinted at earlier (spoilers, sorry), nothing much happened until the end of the day. Which turned out to be about two hours later than we'd planned, because when we tried to close up the doors at five o'clock, the waiting queues of people threatened to revolt.

It was nearly seven, then, when something like serenity finally descended. Relatively speaking. We had only about thirty people left in the hall, and most of them had already viewed the Wand. Many of them were clustered together in knots, talking excitedly — about the Wand, about its rumoured history, but most of all about Merlin.

Everyone is fascinated with Merlin.

Feeling myself justified in deserting my post, I sidled up to Jay. 'On a scale of one to ten, how knackered are you?'

'About eleven, but this is a meaningless measure.'

'Oh? Why?'

He looked at me. 'If you aren't exhausted, you aren't trying hard enough.'

'All work and no play makes Jay a dull boy.'

He snorted.

'And in due course a burned-out boy.'

'Hasn't happened yet.'

'Therefore it's impossible.'

He gave an affirmative nod.

'Nonetheless, would you maybe consider that dinner thing sometime soon? I at least would prefer not to starve to death in pursuit of a thief.'

'Nancy Drew would be ashamed of you.'

'But I think Bess would totally get me.'

He grinned. 'I am hungry,' he admitted.

'The man admits a weakness!'

'I shan't make a habit of it. You'd never respect me again.'

'I'll ask Rob to turf these fine people out,' I said. 'Time to close—'

And I stopped, because at last, guys, something *happened*. I won't admit to having felt a sense of disappointment at the uneventful day we'd had; all we'd done all day was herd people about, and answer the same questions over and over again with the same pack of lies. It made me happy I hadn't ended up as an events planner for real.

Well, our patience paid off. And *then* some.

Sort of.

I hadn't stopped speaking because anything especially dramatic happened. It was only that I'd noticed another visitor, someone I'm certain hadn't been in the room five minutes before. We'd shut the double doors by then in an attempt to stem the tide, and I hadn't noticed them opening. Apparently the duo of Rob's people stationed either side of the doorway hadn't noticed them opening, either.

Nonetheless, here was someone new. She was standing right in front of the glass case containing the Wand, inspecting it with narrow-eyed attention, and the reason I was so entirely fascinated by this circumstance was that the case was open.

The case was open.

Like she'd just lifted the lid, casual as you please, never mind the fact that it was securely locked and bristling with sealed-for-all-of-time-don't-even-try charms.

Following the line of my gaze, Jay froze. Both of us stared, dumbfounded, at the newcomer for several seconds.

She, unperturbed or oblivious, dipped a hand into the case and drew out the Wand.

'Um,' I said, mobilising myself. 'Excuse me?'

She didn't look up.

'*Excuse* me,' I said again, walking over. I caught Rob's eyes and attempted a frantic *get-over-here* signal with my own. 'Please don't touch the Wand,' I said, stupidly, for here was our thief; she already had her mitts all over our contraband; and all I could think of to say was *please don't touch*?

Please don't somehow circumvent the best magickal security known to man or beast and vanish without trace?

Please don't shame the entire Society and all my friends with a flick of your impossibly powerful fingers, tearing our brilliant plan into tatters in the process?

Please get the hell out of my exhibition hall — but slowly, leaving Rob and team plenty of time to pursue?

Finally, she looked up, and stared directly at me. She wasn't much to look at, truth be told, by which I mean that there was nothing about her to suggest that she might be the most powerful magician in the known world. She looked a ways younger than my not-at-all-doddery sprig-gan persona, though by no means young. She had rather swarthy skin, white hair, and keen, amber-hazel eyes, with the kind of proud, straight-backed posture most of us lose by the age of thirty. She wore a simple black coat with a dark blue dress underneath, and shabby, well-loved black boots. She could have been anyone at all, in short — except for one thing.

When I got closer to her, I felt something unusual about her. A restless, roiling aura of pure magick, I realised with a shock — just the kind of thing you feel if you're crazy or stupid enough to get close to a griffin. Or a unicorn. It wasn't in-your-face obvious; quite subtle, really. But I'm used to Addie by now; I *have* been stupid enough to hobnob with a bunch of griffins; and since our trip to Vale, I've developed a little bit of the same thing myself.

In my case, it's kind of stuck on, like wrapping paper, which is why I periodically have to go take a horn holiday. And why I sometimes magick-zap things that I touch, if I get excited about something.

In this woman's case, it felt... normal. Like having brown hair, or green eyes; nothing anyone would think remarkable.

So this wonder of nature and magick looked right at me, and said: 'This is pretty work.'

Rob had reached us by this time, and stood looming at the woman's elbow. Most of his team were coming towards us, forming a ring around the case and the woman holding the Wand, ready to cut off her escape. 'Put the Wand down, ma'am,' he said firmly.

'But,' she said, ignoring him, 'it isn't mine.'

And she put it back, quietly closed the case, and turned away.

Jay's eyebrows shot up, and I realised it wasn't because of what the woman had said. It was because the charms on the case were back, as strong as ever, like they'd never disappeared. He tried the lid; it was locked again, too.

Somehow, in that moment, I lost track of the woman.

So did Rob. 'Where is she?' he barked, looking wildly around. He issued a few orders, and his subordinates — John, Dylan, and Rebecca, some of them; I didn't know everybody's names — fanned out across the hall, Wands raised.

They didn't find her.

I did.

'*There*,' I gasped, spotting her quite on the other side of the hall. Three steps would carry her out of the doors, at which point she would no doubt vanish forever.

'Wait!' I shouted, and took off at a dead run, heedlessly shoving people out of my way as I went. 'I need to talk to you!'

She kept walking. In no hurry at all, mind; measured steps, like she had nothing to worry about from us. Which, clearly, she didn't.

'I just want to talk!' I yelled, mustering a final burst of speed.

Somehow, I never reached her. I should have. I was really moving, short legs notwithstanding, and she was strolling along like she had all the time in the world.

But my last few strides got me nowhere. I remained two or three steps away, unable to close the distance between us.

She did pause, though, and gave me another of those hard stares. What she was seeing in me, I could have no idea; she hadn't looked at anybody else quite like that.

In fact, come to think of it, she hadn't looked at anybody else at all.

'Please,' I panted. 'Nobody wants to harm you. But I desperately need to ask you a question.'

Make that about fifty questions, starting with "did you pinch Merlin's grimoire", going on to "what did you *mean,* that Wand isn't yours?" and ending with "who in the ever-living hell are you anyway?".

She released me from her scrutiny, and turned away.

Then she was gone. I glimpsed, or I *thought* I glimpsed, a section of the doors dissolving into nothing for a split second — sort of like that trick Jay did that one time, when he opened what he called a "void" through a certain impassable object — but the impression was so fleeting, I couldn't be sure.

Either way, she was gone.

I stopped trying to run, and stood, panting for breath and grappling with my dismay.

We'd lost her.

Jay came up, and stood in silence for a while, staring at the firmly closed doors as helplessly as I was. Rob's team went past us at a run and poured out of the doors in pursuit, but somehow I knew it was hopeless. She wasn't there to find.

Finally Jay said, 'I guess we found our purloiner of grimoires.'

I nodded. There could be no doubt. All the vaunted security at the Elvyng manor would be as nothing to someone with skills like that. We no longer needed to waste our time working out how someone had managed to pass through it.

There had been something about this woman, too, that suggested she was... above such mundane considerations as locked doors, security charms (and alarms), and indeed the law. Like she existed outside all of that, on some other plane of reality altogether. She wouldn't hesitate to stroll into William Elvyng's house and wander out with Merlin's Grimoire tucked under her arm.

'Question though,' I said. 'She declined the Wand because it's not hers.'

'Right.'

'But if we're right, and she's our thief... she took the grimoire.'

'Which wasn't hers either. So why was that different?'

I swallowed. 'Jay. This is going to sound crazy—'

'What else is new?'

Hah. 'What if she took the grimoire because it *was* hers?'

And there was that are-you-freaking-crazy stare again. '*Hers*? Surely you aren't saying...'

'I think,' I said slowly, appalled by the enormity of what I was about to say. 'I think we just met Merlin.'

10

'Setting aside for a moment the extreme improbability that Merlin ever existed in the first place,' said Jay, 'a fact which no one has any real evidence for, nothing but old stories—'

'There's lots of truth in old stories,' I objected.

'Yes, but also lots of nonsense, and a story isn't evidence of anything.'

'Fair enough.'

'Setting that aside,' he repeated. 'Those stories go back, what, a thousand years at least? How could Merlin still be alive?'

'Improbably powerful magician,' I said.

'And?'

'You did see her breeze past our best security like it was nothing? And you can't have forgotten Farringale, either. Baroness Tremayne? The echoes? It wouldn't even be the first time we've encountered someone who absolutely shouldn't still be alive anymore.'

'True,' said Jay, but sceptically.

'And before you feel it necessary to point out that this Merlin is female, we also have no evidence that Merlin was male, either. Just stories, many of them written well after the age of Merlin, and largely penned by men.'

'Who might edit the gender of the hero of the story because of... reasons?'

I shrugged. 'Nothing so nefarious. They might simply have... assumed.'

Jay sighed. 'I concede that there's something in what you say. And you might be right.'

'Wow,' I said. 'Thanks.'

'But it's crazy beyond all reason and we have no proof.'

'What's your guess?' I said. 'If she isn't Merlin, who is she?'

Jay had nothing to say.

He tried, poor boy. His mouth opened, and I could practically see the gears whirring in his brain as he sought for another, more reasonable theory than mine.

But it would all be the merest guess-work, and he knew it. He gave up. 'I don't know,' he said. 'What's worse, I have no idea how we're going to find out.'

A lowering reflection, that. Our maybe-Merlin had disappeared out of our lives in the blink of an eye, and even I wasn't crazy enough to imagine we could somehow track her down. Where would we even start? How could we expect to find any trace of a person who could glide through doors, and ignore the Society's most powerful magicks as easily as she might ignore a fly?

'So we're stumped,' I said.

'Yep.'

I turned and surveyed what was left of our exhibition. Our remaining visitors were all gathered around the case, talking excitedly; word of our maybe-Merlin's feats of aborted thievery would spread far and wide after today. Rob and team were still engaged in their futile attempt to chase down our suspect. Various of our friends and colleagues from the Society were drifting about or slumped against walls, looking as tired and disappointed as I felt.

Yep, this was an epic fail.

'Let's get this lot out of here,' I said, drawing myself up. 'And then we're going to dinner.'

'Right,' said Jay tiredly, and strode off in the direction of the Wand-case.

'And it had better be a *big* dinner,' I added to his retreating back.

In the end, I didn't even eat much of our admittedly enormous repast.

I know. *Me,* Ves, lacked appetite, despite the small army of delicious dishes Jay and I had splurged on between us.

We'd been too tired, and too distracted, to faff about picking somewhere nice. So we'd headed for the nearest pub, and finding their menu replete with delicious stuff we had gone a bit nuts. We had deep-fried brie and baked camembert (Jay's choices, proving himself a cheese connoisseur). We had a deep bowl piled high with heavily salted chips (my choice, proving myself not entirely uninfluenced by Addie). We had battered fish and peas, some excellent fresh bread, and a plate of raspberry cheesecake.

I attacked this feast with gusto at first, but rising nausea forced me to slow down to bird-like mouthfuls.

'Are you okay?' said Jay after a while, watching my lack of progress with sharp eyes.

'Sick,' I said.

'As in, ill?' Jay looked aghast.

'No, no,' I said quickly. 'I just feel... weird.' I shifted in my chair, too restless to sit still, despite my exhaustion.

'It's been a weird day,' Jay offered. 'And it's possible to be too tired to eat.'

I nodded, though without fully agreeing with him. He was right, but I felt that my disorder, somehow, had something to do with Merlin. It had begun around the second time she had pinned me with that piercing gaze, as though something about that look had mixed up my insides.

And I was ferociously zapping everything I touched, which didn't help. I speared a chip with my fork; *zap*. I gave up on the fork, and used my fingers instead; *zzap*. I picked up my glass of beer and took a swallow; *zzzap-ap*, and also STARS.

Pretty.

Disconcerting.

'You definitely aren't right,' said Jay, having watched in silence as my rain of sparkly stars wafted over the table.

'Tell me about it,' I said. 'But never mind me. What are we going to do about Merlin?'

'Nothing,' said Jay glumly.

'Defeatist.'

'I know, but I can't think of a damned thing. Can you?'

I had to sigh. 'No. And how galling is that? Mission accomplished, thief identified, fat lot of good it does us.'

'I suppose it's possible this woman wasn't the same person who stole the grimoire?' Jay said.

'It's possible,' I said tonelessly. 'But not likely. Who else do you suppose is out there, fixated upon Merlin's personal odds-and-bobs and impossibly great at making off with them? Whoever took the grimoire left *no* clues. No signs of a break-in, no traces of a struggle with the case it was in. No evidence of how they got out again. And that has to be because they didn't use the locks, and they weren't affected by the magick. They — *she* — just walked in, picked up the book, and walked out again. Who else could do that?'

Jay's turn to sigh. 'I can't think of a reason why you're wrong there.'

'Makes a change.'

'Question,' said Jay.

'Great.'

'Why'd this woman show up at our exhibition when she did? She needn't have attracted any attention. She could have gone in after we'd closed up and left.'

'The Wand wouldn't have been there. We would've taken it away with us.'

'Yes, but how could she know that?'

I shrugged. 'She might guess that. Wouldn't be hard.'

'Right. Or she might have had some other reason for showing up when she did.'

'Like what?'

'Maybe she was curious about who had the Wand.'

'Curious?'

'She looked rather hard at you,' said Jay, suiting action to words, and looking rather hard at me too.

'You noticed that too, huh?' I avoided Jay's eyes, and looked at the table.

'And now you're spewing stars over the table and fizzing like a popped bottle of bubbly.'

I tried a smile. 'You say that like it's a bad thing.'

Jay didn't say anything for a while.

I picked at a couple of abandoned chips.

'Well, never mind me,' I said eventually. 'We need a plan of action.'

Jay still didn't speak. He had stopped eating too, and sat fiddling with his fork. Sneaking a glance at his face, I found him gazing at nothing, typically unreadable.

'The Wand lost her interest almost immediately,' said Jay. 'Overall, she seemed far more interested in *you.*'

I couldn't disagree, unaccountable as it was.

'So if that was Merlin,' Jay continued. 'She must have known in advance that the Wand wasn't hers. Right?'

'Unless she's lost a Wand, somewhere back in the mists of time, and hoped this one was it.'

'Unlikely. There are too many coincidences in that.'

'And we've been spreading pictures of the thing everywhere. If she heard about the exhibition, she'd have had chance to see a picture, too.'

Jay nodded. 'And the chances of Indira's design happening to match any Wand of hers exactly are so small, it has to be impossible.'

I sat up a bit. 'So she knew the Wand wasn't hers. Why then did she come? Apparently it wasn't to issue us with a cease-and-desist notice.'

'Right. She didn't seem to care that we were passing off a Wand as hers — or Merlin's — and if she's half as good as she seems to be, she must've realised, as soon as she saw it, that it was a new creation.'

'So she didn't come by to collect her Wand, or to lay the smackdown on us for fraud.'

'She was interested,' said Jay.

'Curious? Really?'

'In who *we* are, and what we're doing.'

'She asked no questions.'

Jay nodded slowly, thinking.

I cudgelled my brains into something resembling coherent thought, too.

At length I said: 'Where might she have gone, when she left the exhibition?'

'If we knew that—'

'Maybe we could guess. If she's half as interested in us as you imagine—'

'In *you*,' Jay corrected.

'—then maybe she hasn't vanished into the mist, never to be seen again, but—'

My phone rang. I'd set it down on the table while I ate, and it vibrated loudly against the polished pine.

All the words I'd been planning to say went straight out of my head when I saw the caller ID.

'It's Milady,' I said dumbly.

Jay's brows went up. 'Okay...?'

I felt frozen. I can't explain why. I had the oddest feeling of a great weight settling upon me, like something was about to happen that would change everything. Forever.

Maybe in ways I didn't want and couldn't cope with.

'Aren't you going to answer it?' said Jay.

I just looked at him, wide-eyed and speechless.

He gave me an odd look, reached slowly past me, and picked up my phone.

'Hi, Milady,' he said. 'Sorry, Ves is having a funny moment. What's up?'

Silence for a few moments.

Jay's brows climbed higher, and then higher again. He blinked.

'Right,' he said at last. 'Right, okay.'

He ended the conversation with, 'On our way,' and hung up.

Silently he returned my phone to its former position beside my plate.

'There's a visitor at Home,' he said calmly. 'She is desirous of seeing you as soon as possible.'

I swallowed a lump in my throat. 'She?' I croaked.

Jay nodded.

He didn't explain further, but he didn't need to.

Whoever it was, Milady thought the situation important enough to haul us straight back Home. That was a first.

Whatever was going on, I was going to have to dig deep, put my Big Girl boots on, and pull myself together.

One way or another, magick needed me.

'Okay,' I said, rising from my chair. I paused to stuff two more chips in my face — if my life was about to be turned upside down, I was going to need sustenance — and collected my paraphernalia. My phone I put in my pocket, where I'd feel it if it rang again. 'It's lucky you're driving,' I said to Jay.

Jay's gaze flicked to my fingers, which at that moment were fizzing so hard with magick I could barely feel the things I'd picked up. I don't know how he could tell, but apparently he could, for he said: 'It is. Come on.'

Out we went to the car park. The bus had already departed, taking the rest of the Society home the slow way. Jay and I had walked down to the pub. I waited while he faffed with his phone, checking the location of the nearest Way-henge.

'Is there an app for that?' I said.

'Yes.' Jay didn't look up.

'What? I was joking.'

'Nonetheless, there is.'

'For the... what, five or so Waymasters in the country?'

'I mean, the world's a bit bigger than that.'

'Sure, but who thought it worth their while to make a whole app for so small a number of people?'

'I did.'

'Uh.'

Jay put his phone away, flashing me a brief smile. 'This way. Come on.'

I thought about what Val had said about Indira. 'We really aren't paying you *or* your sister enough.'

'Says who?'

'I'm not sure we *can* pay you enough.'

Jay shrugged. 'We've turned down better offers to be here.'

'Don't leave me?' I cleared my throat. 'Us, I meant. Please don't leave *us*.'

Jay cast me a swift, sideways glance. 'Certainly not for money.'

'For something else?'

He thought. 'Probably not.'

And I had to be satisfied with that.

11

I HAD SO CONFIDENTLY expected to find Merlin waiting for us at Home, I was surprised speechless to discover Sally instead.

At first, I thought maybe there had been a mistake. We were sent to one of the smaller (and more secret) meeting-rooms on the ground floor, and when I saw Sally (the fence, remember?) sitting alone at the glass-topped table with a cup of coffee before her, and an open notebook, I conducted a quick sweep of the room. You know, just in case an entire extra person was sitting in one of the other chairs, or upon the window-seat, and I'd somehow failed to notice.

It was just Sally.

She looked up as we came in, and greeted us with one of those professional nods that always seem just a bit grim. 'I apologise for the lateness of the hour,' she said. 'I understand you have been much engaged on business today.'

'To say the least,' I sighed, sliding into a chair opposite her. 'But we appreciate your coming by. I gather you have news? Something important?'

She nodded. 'I've already seen Val. She thought you should hear it directly from me.'

'Sounds serious.'

Sally glanced at her page of notes. 'It is about the matter of Merlin's Grimoire.'

'You've discovered something?'

She hesitated. 'In a manner of speaking.'

We waited.

'I sent out enquiries,' she began. 'Among various of my contacts who might have heard about that incident. To my surprise, I found that several had. It had never reached *my* ears because the stories had been broadly dismissed as moonshine. And they do sound improbable. I would have dismissed them myself, were it not for your information.'

'Let me guess,' I said. 'A shadow in the night? An improbably successful super-thief who can bypass security like it was never there, help themselves to the most carefully guarded artefacts, and vanish without trace, leaving not a single clue behind?'

Sally stared at me.

'And this super-villain primarily targets Merlin-related objects?'

'Exactly.' Sally closed her notebook with a *snap*. 'If you already knew about this, why did you—'

'We didn't,' I said. 'We found out about it today.'

Jay added, 'It's been an interesting day.'

'Tell me,' said Sally.

So we did, though we left out the parts about the maybe-Merlin eyeballing *me* like I was relevant to something. 'We have no idea who she is,' I finished. 'Except that she talked like she *is Merlin*, and we know that must be impossible.'

'That, too, I've heard,' said Sally. 'I don't think anyone believes it.'

Jay and I exchanged a look.

'You mean you *do*?' said Sally in disgust.

'Not... exactly,' I said. 'But there's clearly something very strange going on here.'

'Strange, and by all logic ought to be impossible,' said Jay.

'Where else has she been seen?' I asked.

'I don't know that there have been too many direct sightings of the thief,' said Sally. 'Besides the grimoire, a belt buckle said to be Merlin's disappeared about two years ago from a private house in Scotland. The thing was inscribed in Ogham, believed to be authentic, as far as anyone can be sure about that. And there was one more rumoured incident, though it was too long ago to be relevant.'

'Maybe not,' I said. 'How long ago?'

'More than twenty years. A chalice, made of horn inlaid with opal and silver, taken from a museum in Cornwall.'

'Silver?' said Jay sharply.

I saw the direction of his thoughts. Was it silver, or argent?

'Why didn't Val find anything about this on the net?' I said, frowning.

'Because there's nothing there,' said Sally. 'Anytime anyone writes anything about this "Merlin", those articles... disappear. It's become something of an urban legend, spread by word-of-mouth.' She smiled briefly. 'I believe some of my people think I may have run mad, asking about folk tales.'

'This is really helpful,' I said. 'Thank you for bringing it to us.'

She nodded. 'I'll let you know if I hear of anything more concrete.'

She waited, expecting something.

'We'll let you know if we do,' I promised.

I guessed right, for she smiled. The curiosity bug had bitten her pretty badly. 'I've got a hot chocolate appointment with Val,' she said, rising from her chair.

'Don't be late,' I said. 'She hates that.'

Sally bustled out fast enough, leaving me to exchange long looks with Jay.

'The plot thickens,' he said.

'The internet is full of references to things Merlin's said to have owned or used at one time or another,' I said. 'Those articles haven't vanished, and neither have the objects.'

'Just the articles pertaining to the things that *were* taken,' said Jay.

'So why those things?'

Jay sighed. 'You're going to argue that it has to be because they're authentic, aren't you?'

'Can you think of another reason?'

'I really can't.'

I looked around at the empty room, feeling slightly deflated. Never mind that we had just received a lot of interesting and relevant information. 'I thought she'd be here,' I said.

'Merlin?'

I nodded.

'I thought she would, too,' Jay admitted. 'Milady didn't say who it was, but she sort of hinted...'

'That it was somebody Secret and Important?'

'Right.'

'Which, I suppose, it was.'

'But,' sighed Jay. 'All Sally's info, while fascinating, still doesn't help us. If all these objects were taken by the same person, no one seems to know where to find her.'

'So we're still stuck.'

'Like glue.'

I held out my closed fist. 'Go Team Magick.'

Jay bumped my fist with his own. 'It's great being un-stoppable.'

I sighed, and lowered my cheek to the table. 'Wake me when we have a break-through.'

Crystobel called me the following morning.

I had occasion to regret that I'd given her my personal mobile number.

'Ms. Vesper?' she said crisply into my ear.

'Ves,' I said. 'Please. Ms. Vesper makes me feel about eighty.'

I suppose my bleatings deserved no particular response; they certainly received none. 'Is there any progress to report?' she said.

'Well...' I debated how much to tell her. 'Sort of?'

'Sort of.'

'We're fairly sure we have identified the person who took the grimoire.'

'Oh!'

'Sort of.' I mean, I would recognise her if I saw her in the street, but that was about it. The only name we had for her was Merlin — maybe — and we had nothing else. Hardly information to take to the police, or indeed to Crystobel Elvyng.

'Perhaps you could explain what you mean?' She spoke civilly enough, but I detected traces of impatience.

Fine, less of the caginess then.

'The likely candidate for the theft of your grimoire identifies herself as Merlin,' I said, and then paused, remembering too late that she hadn't actually done so. We had, as the only interpretation we could come up with for her minimal utterances that made any sense.

Sort of.

There was silence on the line.

'So you're saying,' she finally began, 'that some Merlin-wannabe has taken my grimoire?'

Curse it, how difficult could a conversation get?

Pretty work, maybe-Merlin had said. *But it isn't mine.*

'I think she may have believed herself to be retrieving her own property,' I said.

'Ah. Bit of a crazy, is it? That can happen,' said Crystobel knowledgeably. 'I trust you'll have her apprehended soon, and the grimoire restored to my father.'

'We're doing our best,' I said weakly. How could I explain the rest? Unless being "a bit of a crazy" could imbue a person with astonishing magickal powers, Crystobel's explanation could be nowhere near the truth. But to say as much would make *me* sound a bit crazy.

We needed something more concrete before I could lay any of this before our client.

So I mouthed a few reassuring words and let her ring off, confident in the belief that her family would have their grimoire back soon.

Hah.

Then I threw in the towel, proverbially speaking, and took myself up to Milady's tower.

It's always humiliating to have to go up there and admit to being clueless, but one must swallow one's pride. Sometimes, a conversation with Milady is exactly what's needed to clear the head.

'So,' I said half an hour later, pacing restlessly back and forth across the plush carpet of Milady's personal (and rather sumptuous) tower chamber. 'We're in a bind. On the one hand, these speculations of ours might well turn out to be moonshine, as Sally put it. They *are* completely bonkers. In which case, we've gone down completely the wrong track, and we will have to go back to square one. On the other hand, we might be absolutely right about this "Merlin" person; but that isn't especially likely, and either way it doesn't help us much if we can't find her.'

'Why isn't it especially likely?' said Milady.

That brought my pacing to a halt. 'Um. Because the figure of Merlin has always been treated as more myth than reality, and even if he — or she — was a real person once, it must be extremely unlikely that he or she could still be alive today.'

'You've encountered such things before.'

'Baroness Tremayne? I had thought of that, but it's different. The Baroness is locked between the echoes of Farringale, whatever that means; I'm still unsure. What it *doesn't* seem to mean is that she's free to wander the streets of the twenty-first century world, alive and kicking, the way this maybe-Merlin is.'

'There could still be another explanation,' said Milady.

'Oh, there *could*,' I agreed. 'But I haven't the faintest idea what it might be; neither does Jay; and that leaves us with no avenue for investigation.'

Milady was silent for a while. I wondered, not for the first time, what might be going through her head. This disembodied-voice thing was difficult. No face to read, no visual cues. Just words, or indeed silence.

'I find myself with a dilemma,' said she, and that wasn't what I was expecting her to say at all.

'Oh?' I said, perking up.

'What you have told me interests me greatly,' she said. 'It is... not what I had imagined you were to find, upon launching this hoax of an exhibition. But I nonetheless find myself unsurprised.'

'You know something about this Merlin?'

This silence was undoubtedly a hesitation. Milady didn't know what to say.

Milady didn't know what to say.

I sensed a secret, and pounced. 'If you know something that has some bearing on this case…' I began, and then had no idea how to finish the sentence. Out with it? Speak up, or suffer the consequences?

'I suppose there is no other way to persuade Ms. Elvyng to part with some of her argent?' said Milady. 'Purchase, for example? I am assured of Mandridore's financial assistance.'

'We could try that, but Jay and I already offered to buy from her. She said she doesn't need more money. She wants her grimoire.'

Milady sighed. 'And if it should prove not to be her grimoire?'

'You mean it really does belong to this woman?'

'Perhaps it might. What then?'

I shook my head. 'I don't know. I cannot imagine Crystobel, or her father, would welcome the idea that they aren't getting their grimoire back, let alone that they never really owned it in the first place. And they'd need concrete proof that the grimoire is the rightful property of this Merlin-woman, and how could we get that?'

Milady addressed none of these obstacles. Instead she said: 'Forgive me if I backtrack, but I thought you implied that this woman evinced a special interest in you, Ves. Am I right to think it?'

My turn to hesitate. 'I might have imagined it,' I said. 'Although Jay got the same impression, so maybe not.'

'What did she say to you?'

'Nothing. She said very little to anybody. She just... looked at me.'

'Looked?'

'In a special way. Like she was trying to read my soul, or like... she saw something really compelling. And she did that more than once.'

'She did not *look* at anybody else in this way?'

'No. Just me.'

Silence again, for a little while. 'I had wondered,' said Milady, but in an abstracted way, as though she were not really talking to me anymore. 'When the lyre...'

'The lyre?' I prompted, when she trailed off.

'Ves,' said Milady, sounding once again like her efficient, no-nonsense self. 'There is more afoot here than I can speak of. I cannot tell you the precise identity of the woman you met, for I'm unsure of it myself. But I urge you to keep an open mind. There is more to magick than you know.'

12

'I'VE CERTAINLY LEARNED *THAT* lately,' I muttered, thinking back over all the bizarre things I'd witnessed in the past year. Jay's Waymastery whizzery, and that thing he did with the voids. Perambulating buildings and a small army of chatty, haunted houses. Alternate Britains drenched in magick. Paintings of long-dead (sort of) people, who talked like they were still alive (which they sort of were). Griffins and Farringale. Turning into a unicorn.

That lyre.

'Can you give us some kind of lead?' I pleaded. 'We just need a direction to go in.'

'It may be that you will not be able to restore this grimoire into the Elvyngs' possession,' said Milady.

'Uh. Then... then what do we do? We need that argent.'

'I can send a negotiator to Ms. Elvyng. Perhaps she can be persuaded to sell the argent, if she is offered a suitable price. If not money, then there may be something else she will find desirable.'

'That could work,' I said, if doubtfully. Crystobel seemed very set on the grimoire. 'What would you like us to do in the meantime?'

'You won't find this Merlin by looking,' said Milady. 'If she wishes to find *you*… she will do so. And I think perhaps she might, Ves.'

'So… we're waiting.'

'Of course, if you have other leads to investigate unrelated to the woman from your exhibition, by all means pursue them.'

We didn't. 'Can I have a chocolate party while I wait?'

I heard the smile in her next words. 'I believe you capable of mustering your own supplies of chocolate by this time, Ves.'

'Yours are better,' I said. Not only did they trounce every other conceivable hot chocolate in consistency and flavour, they also had a way of making you feel better. Plus, they were a display of Milady's approval, like a gold star from your primary-school teacher (or a unicorn sticker, on one memorable occasion in my personal history). What's not to love?

'Very well,' said Milady. 'You'll find a pot by your chair in the first-floor common room. Jay is waiting for you.'

Down I went, feeling rather predictable, but honestly not minding very much.

It wasn't quite true that Jay was waiting for me. He was there, to be sure, slouched in his Jay-chair, but since he evinced zero interest in my appearance I couldn't imagine him to be missing me very much. When my cheery greeting went unanswered I sat quietly down, and sipped chocolate in silence.

He didn't move, not for ten minutes. Then suddenly he stirred, as though waking from a weird open-eyed slumber, and looked at me. Startled, like I'd just popped up out of thin air. 'Ves,' he said.

'Hi!' I said. 'I've been here a while?'

'Sorry, I was... thinking.' He sat up a bit, snagged the rest of the chocolate (to my mild regret) and downed half the cup in one gulp.

'About?'

'The grimoire, mostly.'

'To any great effect?'

'If you mean have I solved the mystery, then no.'

'Damnit.'

'But I did have some new thoughts.'

'I like New Thoughts!'

He grinned at me. 'You might not like these.'

'Hit me with them. I'm a big girl, I can take it.'

'Well.' Jay tugged gently on the end of his own nose, a weird/adorable habit I've noticed in him before when he's thinking. I wonder if it helps? 'There was a question I was asking myself,' he said, and then stopped talking again.

'Okay! Ask me this question too.'

'You'll probably think it's stupid.'

'You're talking to crazy-idea Ves, remember? Something's being merely *stupid* is no bar whatsoever to its also being brilliant.'

'Good point.'

'Jay,' I said wearily, when he still didn't speak. 'Spit it out. It can't be that bad.'

'How do we know the grimoire was even stolen?' he said.

'Uh... because its owners told us as much?'

'How do they know it was stolen?'

'...because it isn't where it's meant to be anymore, and neither of them removed it?'

'So we know that it's missing from its case,' Jay said. 'That's all. We don't *know* that it was taken out of the case and the building by a thief, because there is no evidence for that. And whatever we may have concluded after meeting that scarily powerful lady at the exhibition, that doesn't necessarily mean that somebody with godlike magickal potency breezed in and extracted it. There could be another explanation.'

I wanted to say, *like what*, with all due scorn, for theft was both the most obvious and the most likely explanation when you're talking about a grimoire that changes hands for unthinkably large sums of money.

But I didn't, because once I thought about it I realised Jay was right. There were other possible explanations, even if they were unlikely. But our current theory was spectacularly unlikely, too, so what did that matter?

'If you want to suggest that the Elvyngs have just mislaid the thing, I'd want to veto that idea,' I said. 'Surely that's impossible.'

'Not impossible,' corrected Jay. 'So improbable as to be *nearly* impossible, but it could happen.'

'All right. I'm putting that one at the bottom of the list.'

Jay nodded. 'It could, by some means or another, still be at the Elvyng residence, most likely without their knowledge.'

'Meaning someone moved it, for motives unknown.'

'Or it moved itself.'

I raised an eyebrow at him.

'We are talking about the personal grimoire of Merlin himself.'

'Or herself,' I said.

'Right.'

'I'm putting that second from the bottom.'

'You think the idea of the grimoire's moving itself around is *less* unlikely than that the Elvyngs clumsily lost it?'

'You've met Crystobel, right?'

He thought that over for a second. 'Good point again.'

I slouched a little deeper in my chair, brain whirring. 'Okay. So it might have moved, or been moved. But why haven't the Elvyngs found it again, in four years?'

'Could be that they simply didn't think to look for it somewhere else in the building. Valuable items kept in glass cases don't tend to just be set down in the wrong place one time, like a bunch of keys.'

'Right, but they have a very capable and knowledge-able butler/housekeeper. Someone would've wondered what this fragile antiquity of a book was doing in the boot-room, halfway down a mountain of mud-crusted wellies.'

Jay winced at that vision of disaster. 'Fair,' he allowed.

'Assuming it was visible to the human eye,' I added.

Jay's turn to blink at me. 'What?'

'Maybe it turned invisible. Merlin's grimoire, remember?'

'I suppose that could be it.'

'It's like Sherlock Holmes said. Once the impossible is eliminated, what remains, however improbable, must be the truth. Or something like that.'

'Neat theory, but we seem to be developing a whole slew of improbable-but-not-quite-impossible ideas.'

'Holmes didn't have to deal with magick,' I agreed. 'In that he had a definite advantage.'

'So an invisible grimoire.'

I nodded. 'It could happen.'

'Why would it be invisible?'

'No idea. Why would it wander out of its protective cabinet?'

'Touché.'

I took a breath. 'And now for the worst idea I've got.'

Jay grimaced. 'On a scale of one to gods-help-me, how bad is it?'

'Bad as in, if I'm right then Crystobel might be taking our eyeballs out with a dessert spoon.'

'Oh god.'

'Okay, so... maybe it doesn't exist anymore. It's gone because it's *gone.*'

'So it literally... what, disintegrated?'

'Could have.'

'I want to ask why.'

'But you won't, because you know I have nothing to tell you.'

'Right.'

'Maybe it lost the will to live,' I mused. 'Separated from its owner and creator, splendidly alone in its isolated kiosk of a library, scarcely ever touched anymore—'

'Ves,' Jay interrupted. 'You're making me feel sorry for a book. Please stop it.'

'Sorry.' I shot out of my chair. 'If we're done theorising about near-impossibilities then we need to go back to William Elvyng's house.'

Jay gazed up at me, and didn't move. 'To do what?'

'To investigate!'

'We've already done that.'

'Yes, but last time we were so certain we were investigating a theft, that's all we looked for. Signs of forced entry or exit, clues as to the *person* who undoubtedly made off with the grimoire. This time's different.'

'I realise, but how are we going to investigate a possible vanishment or disintegration? What clues do you suppose those would leave behind?'

I wilted a bit, deflated. 'You're right, but... then what? How do you propose to determine whether these ideas are correct, if we can't investigate?'

Jay groaned. 'I don't know. We're the worst detectives ever.'

I stood where I was, furiously racking my brains. 'What would Sherlock have done?'

'He would have noticed some small, but profoundly important clue, known immediately what it portended, and have had the mystery solved by tea-time,' said Jay glumly.

'You know, I'm not sure I'm liking this new, defeatist Jay.'

'Ouch.'

'Sorry.'

'It's okay. I'm not loving him either.'

'Em Rogan,' I said.

'What?'

'Clues,' I said intelligently.

I saw light dawn in Jay's eyes. 'Right! If anything magickal happened to the grimoire—'

'Then someone with the right kind of sensitivities might be able to tell us what it was. Or if not that, at least she could tell us *if* something of a magickal nature happened. And since it's hopeless to ask my mother for help, maybe we could borrow Em again.'

'Is it hopeless?' I didn't like the searching look that went with the question.

'She's always far too busy.'

'So you won't even ask?'

'She'll say no.'

'Ves.'

'Mm?'

'Are you afraid to ask?'

I scoffed. 'Afraid? Of my own mother? Ridiculous.'

'Forgive me,' Jay said. He sat shifting in his seat, and well he might, raising such uncomfortable topics. 'But I realise you're used to your mother's saying no to you a lot. I can understand that it hurts.'

'It doesn't hurt,' I muttered, stung. 'She's just a busy person, that's all. I'm fine with it.'

Jay's smile was gentle and understanding and I felt a brief, but intense, desire to punch him. 'Then there can be no harm in asking, can there? You never know, she might say yes.'

'We don't need her to say yes. We can call Em.'

'Emellana Rogan is an important member of the Court at Mandridore. She's also a busy person, and we've far less right to call on her than we have to call on your mother.'

I sought in vain for another reasonable objection to raise. I realised, dimly, that I had a far greater desire to see Em again than to see my mother Delia, and my mind shied away from examining why that might be. I only suffered a vague sense of guilt.

But what was I worried about? Calling my mother could have only one outcome. She'd say no, waspishly and definitively, and that would be that.

Then we could call Em anyway.

'All right,' I said, and with saintly smile and angelic demeanour — I deserved serious points for tractability, didn't I? — I took out my mobile and dialled my mother's number.

Any hopes I had that she might not even answer died away on the second ring. 'Hello?' she said, sounding, for once, fairly chirpy.

'Mum,' I said. 'It's me. You busy?'

'Always.'

Promising. 'Jay and I could use your help.'

A sigh. 'With what?'

'We're trying to trace a lost grimoire for the Elvyngs and we think something—'

'The *Elvyngs*?' she all but shrieked in my ear. 'You're working for the Elvyngs?'

'Temporarily...'

'Giddy gods.'

I swallowed. 'You, uh, know them?'

'I know *of* them,' she said, and added acidly, 'I'm not exactly the type to be on a first-name basis with magickal celebrities.'

'Mum, you're the queen of an Yllanfalen kingdom.'

A pause. 'I'd forgotten that for a second.'

'So anyway, we're—'

She went on as though I hadn't spoken. 'They're amazing. They've funded half of the most successful digs in recent history. Clamberwelle. Torrington. The Draypool Chalice was rediscovered because of them. Hell, Claud

Elvyng was among the most prominent and successful magickal archaeologists in history. The things that man pulled out of the ground in the twenties—'

'Mum.' I thought it wise to cut her off, or she might bang on about it all day. 'William Elvyng's lost an important grimoire, his daughter Crystobel has hired us to find it, and we've a theory we want to investigate. We need someone who—'

'Crystobel Elvyng? You've spoken to Crystobel Elvyng?'

'Yes, we—'

'I'll help.'

'What?' I said numbly.

'What do you need me to do?'

'Er, we want to go back to the Elvyng residence and check for magickal residue in the—'

'The Elvyng *house*?'

'Yes...'

There followed an odd, sucking-in noise, which I interpreted as my mother trying not to scream with excitement. 'I'm there,' she said. 'I'll meet you there.'

'I thought you said you were busy?'

'Never too busy to spare time for my daughter,' she said primly.

Uh huh. 'If you can meet us there tomorrow,' I suggested, realising she'd have farther to travel than we did, and no convenient Waymaster to hand. 'That'd be great. I'll check with Mr. Elvyng, text you the time later.'

My mother, irascible and pragmatic Delia Vesper, *may* actually have squealed. I think that's what that muffled, covering-the-phone-to-preserve-dignity noise was.

I tried to ignore Jay smirking at me as I hung up the phone.

'See?' he said. 'That wasn't so hard.'

I thought about explaining the fact that the hard part would happen tomorrow, when I had to spend hours in my mother's company and she in mine. But that smug look on his face didn't deserve much of a response, so I merely said: 'I'm going to the library,' and left him to congratulate himself alone.

13

WHEN WE PULLED UP in William Elvyng's driveway at two o'clock the following afternoon, we found my respected parent already present. She sat in the driving-seat of a beaten-up red Peugeot that looked about five hundred years old, tapping her fingers against the steering wheel and generally radiating impatience.

'Mum,' I said, when we had clambered out of our respective cars. 'I thought you'd have a driver.'

Her missing hand was looking way better than it had the last time I'd seen her. It had healed pretty well, and was now a neat, rather than a bloodied, stump. Being Delia, she was totally unselfconscious about it, which was good. But ignoring it to the point of driving herself around one-handed might, I thought, be carrying insouciance a bit far.

'Why would I want a driver?' she said, apparently deciding not to hug me.

I gestured awkwardly in the direction of her missing hand, a hint she either missed entirely or chose to ignore.

When the awkward silence stretched, I changed the subject, Delia-style, by finding something else to criticise. 'Or if there's no gilded carriage for the queen of Ygranyllon, maybe a new car?'

'What's wrong with Bert?' She patted the bonnet of her disreputable banger with marked affection. 'Solid car. Been with me for years.'

'I can see that,' I said.

Jay smoothly intervened. 'Hello, Mrs. Vesper. Nice to see you again.'

'Not married,' she said shortly. 'But yes, lovely.'

Jay looked rather at a loss.

'Just call her Delia,' I said. 'Everyone does.'

Poor Jay's face said, *but she's the queen.*

'Right, Mum?' I prompted.

She smiled in a silky way. 'Queen Delia.'

I snorted. 'She's waiving her right to *your majesty,* just for you.'

'Hey,' said mother. 'I've never been queen of *anything* before. Let me have this.'

'How you've suffered,' said I.

'Coming from the future queen of Mandridore, that's rich.'

'Mum, there is a future queen of Mandridore and it isn't me. Can we move on?'

'Right.' Marching to William Elvyng's door, Delia rang the bell in what Oscar Wilde would describe as a Wagnerian manner.

The butler/housekeeper, whose name I confess to having forgotten, opened it almost immediately.

And then, to my supreme irritation, he bowed low to my mother and said, 'Your Majesty of Ygranyllon. What an honour,' and stood back to hold the door wide for her.

To Jay and I he was merely polite. 'Miss Vesper, Mr. Patel. Welcome back.'

'I've changed my mind,' I whispered, as my mother swept past the butler with head held high. 'I want to be queen of my own faerie kingdom.'

'You had the option,' said Jay. 'You declined, remember?'

'I know! What was I thinking!'

'You were thinking sane and sensible things like, Cordelia Vesper isn't really queen material.'

'Ouch. Are you saying I'd be a bad queen?'

'I think I'm saying you have more important things to do.'

'Than ruling a *kingdom*?'

'We're trying to bring back magick for *all* the kingdoms.'

I stood a bit taller. 'You're right. Excellent pep talk, Mr. Patel.'

'Too kind, your honourary majesty.'

We were conducted into the same, lovely room as before, and found our host ensconced in the same armchair by the fire. He greeted my mother with a bit less reverence than had his butler, to my relief and (perhaps) my mother's chagrin.

Just as well, really, for the moment she found herself in august company she apparently lost the power of speech, and became her brusque, largely silent self. She was almost snappish with poor Mr. Elvyng, and took the seat he offered her with an expression bordering upon a scowl.

I thought about issuing the Elvyngs with a Delia Vesper Manual, but it was a bit late by then.

'So good of you to see us again,' I said to the Elvyng patriarch, trying not to make up for my mother's manner with a flood of gushing.

He inclined his head, quite gracious. 'I understand you have some new ideas to pursue?'

'Yes. It occurred to us — well, to Jay, in fact — that we had previously been so set upon a certain interpretation of events as to ignore other possibilities. We've brought Ms. Vesper—' (No way was I referring to her as Queen Delia) '—because she has a pronounced sensitivity to past magicks, and may be able to tell us if anything unusual, and of a magickal nature, might have happened regarding the grimoire.'

'You have some precise theory, or...?'

'Nothing concrete,' I said, unwilling to expound upon our mad-sounding ideas until we had some kind of supporting evidence. 'We'd just like to experiment with a few possibilities.'

'Of course,' he said. 'Please feel free. Mr. Baker will conduct you to whichever parts of the house you will need to review.' He turned his attention to my mother, and said: 'It is gracious of your majesty to grant us some of your time, and the use of your skills.'

I held my breath, hoping Mum would find something socially acceptable to say.

This one time, she didn't disappoint. 'It is my very great pleasure,' she declared, and if the sentiment was expressed with a fraction too much gracious condescension, I'd take it. It was better than a brusque nod and a grunt of assent, which would be very characteristic.

Off we trailed, then, to the Grimoire Room — after a closing round of smiling pleasantries, of course, some of which might even have been sincere. The obliging Mr. Baker (I remembered!) let us in, and hovered again by the door.

'Right,' I said, all business. 'Mum, do your thing!'

'My thing,' she said, glowering. 'More specifically?'

'Not your gracious queenly thing but your archaeology thing.' Helpfully, I wiggled my fingers in illustration of my meaning.

She rolled her eyes at me, and turned away. 'I can't believe I'm in the Elvyng abode,' she said, somewhat but not entirely *sotto voce.* 'To think, Claud Elvyng probably stood on this very spot.'

'Dignity, Mum. You're a queen, remember?'

Her shoulders straightened. 'Right. Quiet then, while I do my *thing.*'

Obedient daughter that I *always* am, I hushed. So did Jay. We busied ourselves conducting a silent and utterly pointless survey of the room, in quest of those very clues which (according to Jay's very reasonable argument) were most unlikely to exist. And we found sod all, how about that? Shocker. I did want to talk to Mr. Baker; it wouldn't hurt to verify just how unlikely it was that the grimoire could still be in the house after all this time. But that could wait until after Mum was done, since she apparently required *complete silence.*

I'd gone from uselessly employed to thoroughly bored by the time she was finished. It wasn't even interesting to watch her work, since the process consisted of wandering around laying her hands on things and closing her eyes, or sitting cross-legged on the floor in apparently deep meditation.

I tried not to sigh too loudly.

At length, she opened her eyes, looked straight at me, and said: 'There's a lot of old magick here.'

'Old as in?'

'*Old*. Ancient. When was this room built?' That last was directed to Mr. Baker, I judged, since her attention snapped to him.

'It was built to house the grimoire, your majesty,' said he. 'It is therefore in the region of thirty years old, so I understand.'

'You weren't here then?'

He looked faintly offended, as well he might. He must have been a child back then, or at best a teenager. 'I have only been employed by Mr. Elvyng for a short time.'

'What I'm driving at,' she said, 'is the age of this *spot*. If this room, and the grimoire, weren't always here, was there something else? Anything that might account for all this residue?'

'I believe not, your majesty,' said poor Mr. Baker, somewhat disconcerted by this barrage of brisk questions. 'If I have understood Mr. Elvyng's occasional comments correctly, nothing of any import occupied this space until the creation of this room.'

'Then we can cautiously conclude that this magick relates to the grimoire,' she said, rising from her semi-recumbent position upon the floor. 'And that, Cordelia, means that the grimoire is probably authentic.'

'You're certain?'

'Reasonably. This isn't modern magick, by any stretch of the imagination. At a guess, I'd say it dates back a thousand years, give or take a century or so.'

I swallowed. 'That's... intense.'

'If it isn't authentic in the sense that it actually belonged to Merlin, it is at least an incredibly compelling copy dating from an approximately contemporary period *to* Merlin. I'll add that there is a depth to it which no modern magician could mimic.'

It took me a second to parse all those convoluted sentences — Mum had forgotten shyness and queenliness both, and got her academic back on — but once I had I was suitably enthused. 'That fits!' I proclaimed.

'What about more recently?' said Jay.

'I'm getting to that,' Mum snapped.

'Right. Sorry.'

'More recent activity is difficult to determine with any certainty. Obviously there are traces of what were probably security-related enchantments, plus some rather confusing dribs and drabs of various and apparently random magicks. I would surmise that Mr. Elvyng, or perhaps his daughter, has stood here at one time or another and played about with the contents of the grimoire.'

How cool, to be an Elvyng, and get to muck about with Merlin's actual spells. I wonder which ones they chose? I wonder if they worked?

Jay was obviously big with questions, but didn't dare interrupt my irascible mother again.

So I did it. 'If I know you, Mum, you're working your way around to a semi-spectacular conclusion.'

'Semi-spectacular?'

'You aren't quite puffed up enough for a full-on spectacular reveal, hence the semi. Whatever you've got is good, but not great.'

'Is that a not-so-subtle way of asking me to get on with it?'

'Yep.'

She sighed. 'My daughter has no sense of theatre,' she informed Jay.

'I'd... politely disagree,' said he, with as much of a smirk as he thought he could get away with in the presence of two Vespers (a tiny one).

'Right, fine,' said Mum. 'Long story short, yada yada, what was probably the last thing of a magickal nature to occur in this room does seem pretty odd.'

'I love odd,' said I.

Mum nodded enthusiastically. 'Partly because of the possible nature of the charm, partly because of the timing.'

'Mum,' I groaned. 'Please. Just tell us.'

'The *timing*,' she said, with a glare at me, 'is strange because whatever it was can't have happened only four years ago, which I gather was the date of the disappearance. If my conclusions are correct, whatever it was occurred rather longer ago than that. Several years at least.'

'Wha?'

'And the charm itself, well... you'll realise this is an imprecise art, and I can never be certain as to the exact nature of any magickal residue.'

'Disclaimer accepted,' I said.

She nodded. 'But my best guess is: it was some kind of gateway.'

I gave myself several seconds to think that over, but no. It still didn't make the least sense. 'Gateway?' I echoed.

Mum merely nodded.

'As in... someone opened a *new* gateway?'

'Possibly. As I said, imprecise.'

'What kind of gateway? Like the one we found under Sheep Island?'

'Cordelia, as I *just* said, I have no idea. This is the best I can do for you.'

'Sorry, sorry. This is great, really.'

'Except there is maybe one more thing.'

I refrained from loudly sighing, and merely raised an eyebrow.

'There's a flavour to this gateway that's reminiscent of all that ancient magick I mentioned.'

'The ancient Merlin magick?'

'*Reminiscent* of, but not necessarily the same.'

'But — that's a millennium old.'

She looked down her nose at me.

'So you mean to say—'

'Suggest,' interrupted Mum. 'Imply. Hint. Not *say-*, with certainty.'

'You mean to suggestimply*hint* that something or some-one, similar to but not the same as this wielder of ancient and profound magicks, came in here rather more than four years ago, and opened a fresh, new gateway. Which no one does anymore because it's beyond the power of modern magick.'

'Maybe.'

'Which suggests, implies and *hints* that this wielder of gate-opening magicks might themselves be a millennium old.'

'Maybe.'

I thought of our maybe-lady-Merlin, and internally sighed. Everywhere we turned, we encountered more wild improbabilities.

'Maybe it's time to forget about what seems possible or impossible,' I muttered. 'Those words are beginning to lose all meaning here.'

'I'm the queen of Ygranyllon,' said Mum, apropos of nothing, but she had a point. A world in which Delia Vesper reigned over a faerie kingdom was already somewhat out of whack.

'If I may raise a problem with this theory?' said Jay.

'Just the one problem?' I said faintly.

'Delia. If you're right, and someone opened a gateway, presumably they used it to swipe the grimoire. And maybe it was this Merlin-person we've already met. But if they did this more than four years ago, how is it that the grimoire didn't go missing immediately?'

'Maybe it did,' I said.

'If it went missing much more than four years ago, they'd have noticed. Surely.'

'Maybe it came back.'

'What?'

'She's right,' said Mum. 'Gateways work both ways.'

'But—'

'Jay, you said yourself that theft might be too simple an explanation.'

'*Why* though?' said Jay. 'You only need to get away with the loot once. Who steals the same thing twice?'

'I don't know, but if we're dealing with someone who may be a millennium old then I don't think we should assume she thinks the way we would.'

Jay inclined his head. Fair enough.

'And it's at least as likely as that the grimoire took itself off. Mum, can you tell if the gateway's still functional?'

'Nope.'

'Because if it is—'

'I know, and I realise this would be useful information, but I can't tell. If it is still functional, we can conclude it hasn't been used for at least four years.'

I went over to the grimoire's long-empty case, and tried the lid. It wasn't locked anymore. There wouldn't be much point.

I don't know why I thought it would be useful to stare soulfully into the depths of the grimoire's cradle; there was nothing there to see. No glimmers of ancient magick, visible to the naked eye. No ghostly fingerprints, tantalising traces of the presence of one of the world's greatest magickal legends. Just a book-sized nook lined in velvet.

Jay came up beside me. 'There's one way to test if a gateway still works,' he said. He took a bunch of keys from his pocket and placed them carefully in the centre of the vacated book-nook.

The three of us waited, breath held, for something spectacular to happen.

Nothing did.

'It was a nice try,' I sighed, and picked up Jay's keys.

My fingers fizzed.

'Ouch,' I yelped, for the keys were burning in my hands. I dropped them; they fell to the floor with a distant clatter.

Blood roared in my ears, and a white mist floated across my vision. I vaguely heard Jay's voice shouting something, and his hands supporting me — was I swooning? But my hand had strayed back into the depths of the grimoire's case, my fingers were splayed over the velvet, and the strange, intense sensation of distilled magick coursing through my system had spread over my whole body.

'*Ves!*' I heard Jay say. '*Let go of the case!*'

But I couldn't. There was no time. A thundering in my ears drowned all sound; dizziness swamped me; nausea rose.

And then, I achieved a spectacular nineteenth-century swoon, straight into the waiting arms of Jay.

Or so I thought.

'Ah,' said a woman's voice, one that I distantly recognised. 'It *is* you.'

14

I DID NOT IMMEDIATELY open my eyes.

Partly because I was experiencing a dislocated feeling of unreality, and I needed to get a grip.

Partly because I was suffering from a strong desire to unburden myself of the breakfast I'd eaten a couple of hours ago (or what was left of it).

There was no way I was going to greet Britain's most famous magician by throwing up all over her shoes.

'Hi,' I finally croaked, and cautiously opened one eye.

Merlin was not bending anxiously — or curiously — over the woman who'd materialised in her living room, as I might have expected. She was on the other side of the room, engaged in something I couldn't see, because her back was turned to me.

When she made no response to my greeting, I took a moment to take stock of where I had ended up.

It wasn't a living room.

Picture to yourself the classic wizard's house. You know the type. The shelves full of bottled liquids? The scuffed wooden floor, the floating candle-lights, the cat?

The massive spell-book open upon a tall oak table?

That's literally where I was. No word of a lie. I felt like I had strayed into some kind of fairy tale theme park, except that the space had none of the polished-and-pristine, freshly-built perfection of a visitor attraction. This was a place in which somebody lived and worked. The shabbiness of the rugs covering the floors proclaimed it, their woad and indigo-blue shades streaked with dirt here and there, and covered in white cat hair. I knew it from the smells that filled the air: herbs fresh and dried, candle wax, new-baked bread, and other things unknown to me.

I knew it from the presence of Merlin herself, who was no actress playing a role. Magick radiated from her in about the same way that light radiates from the sun.

'So,' I said thickly, once I'd achieved a kneeling position without keeling over. 'This is where the grimoire's got to.'

Her head came up. 'What's that?' she said to the wall, then swiftly turned around. She stared; not at me, but at the spell-book lying open upon the table nearby. And what a spell-book! A proper grimoire, bound in hide, with pages stacked a foot thick.

'Is that still there?' she said, and came over, wiping her hands upon the rough canvas apron she wore.

I managed to beat her to it, but not by much. I had time to observe a two-page spread, closely written in script I could not, at a glance, read, and an astonishing quantity of dust, some of which flew into the air in a thick cloud when the grimoire disappeared.

Which it did instantly, accompanied by a neat little *pop* of magick.

'I had forgotten it,' said Merlin, frowning. But the frown cleared when she looked at me.

I preferred the frown, I quickly decided. She was looking at me the way she had done at our exhibition, only this time it was worse. My insides turned over, and I retched.

'Please,' I said. 'Could we hold off on that for a bit? I am still feeling discombobulated.'

'Ah,' she said.

'Something about being hauled a millennium back in time. It appears it doesn't agree with me.'

She smiled faintly, and went back to her corner work-station. Some of the candles followed her, their flames helpfully brightening as they drifted nearer to her table. 'We have not gone back in time. We have only taken a small step outside of it.'

'Out of time,' I repeated, fuzzily attempting to focus on the concept. 'You mean, between the echoes?'

She looked at me again, over her shoulder. 'Where did you hear of that?'

'They do it at Farringale.' I wanted to go over and see what she was doing, but I felt uncharacteristically diffident. Surely it would be rude to go nosing into the doings of Merlin? *The* Merlin. Giddy gods. 'But it's nowhere near as advanced as this,' I offered, like she would care for my praise.

It was true, though. Baroness Tremayne's hideaway had felt distanced from reality; hazy, echoing, shadowy. In there, you really felt her isolation from the real world, her distance from anything that might pass for living. She was a single thread from a vanished past, slowly unravelling.

Merlin's wizardly wonder could not have been further removed from that. It was vibrantly real, every inch of it, and Merlin herself as alive as you or I.

'Hmm. Perhaps they need help,' she murmured, mostly to herself. She returned to me, but this time she carried a little tincture bottle of smoky glass, inside which bubbled a freshly-poured potion. An actual potion.

We don't really do potions anymore. I mean, we do, but the delivery system's changed. Orlando's lab produces them in handy spherical capsules, the jelly coated ones. You swallow them like a pill (or you burst them in an assailant's face, as per those sleep-bubbles I like so much).

They aren't half so potent as Merlin's. Not even Orlando's can quite match hers. As I downed a real, honest-to-gods potion, for the first time in my life, I experienced a rush of energy so powerful I shrieked a little bit.

'Sorry,' I said, clapping a hand over my mouth.

'Too much?' she said, the frown reappearing.

'I think I'm okay,' I said, drawing in a shaky breath. And I was. More okay than I'd been at any time in my life. More okay than I, probably, ever would be again.

I could get used to it.

'I don't suppose I could get the recipe?' I ventured.

Her smile was brief and sort of... dusty, but it was a smile. 'In a manner of speaking.'

She went back to her work station.

What did that mean? I hadn't quite the gumption to ask. Yes, foolish as hell, but answer me this: would *you* want to look like an idiot in front of *the* Merlin?

So I dithered. My thoughts returned to Jay and Mum, who patently weren't coming in here after me. Then to the grimoire, which had taken my vacated place in the outside world, perhaps forever. Mr. Elvyng would be happy to have it back, to be sure. Would Mum or Jay mind very much that I was gone?

'I hate to bother you,' I said into the silence. 'I, um, didn't quite mean to end up here. We were just looking for the grimoire.'

'I had cause to consult it,' she said, without turning around. Then, vaguely, 'I cannot now remember why.'

And she'd forgotten to return it. It had sat on her table, gathering dust, for who-knew-how-long in her echo of a world. About four years, in our time.

'But why return it?' I said. 'If it's yours? Why not just keep it?'

'It is not mine, precisely, and I rarely have need of it.'

....okay.

'Was that the question you wanted to ask me?' she said.

I thought frantically, trying to remember what had mattered to me a day or two ago. 'Sort of. We were charged with recovering the grimoire, and when I met you the other day I thought you might have it. And you did.'

No response.

'But now I have a million more questions.'

Silence, which I hoped was an invitation to ask some of them.

'Starting with...' I paused, and groped for the gumption I knew I still possessed. Somewhere, deep down. 'Are you... Merlin?'

Her posture changed. Some tension in the shoulders, a rigidity in her stance. I sensed that she was... thinking. Weighing up what to say.

'My name is Ophelia,' she said.

'Ah... oh.' I felt my cheeks turn the colour of a telephone box.

Yep, we were idiots.

'But in the sense that you mean it, yes,' she went on. 'I am Merlin.'

'Ah... okay?' I swallowed. 'Um, how does that work?'

'Where do you see yourself in ten years' time?'

Question number two of twelve million, and already she was dodging.

'Uh?' I said, at my most intelligent.

'Ten years,' she repeated, the words emerging thinly over the clatter of metal against ceramic. She was mixing something. Another potion?

I croaked something vague and idiotic. Ten years? How did I know? I'd be over forty. Probably still single, probably still working for the Society. Doing the same job.

Still happy, I hoped.

But how could Ophelia-Merlin be interested in any of that?'

'I don't know,' I said. 'Probably exactly where I am now.'

'No,' she said firmly. 'You have changed, Cordelia Vesper. You know that you have, though you may not realise how much.'

'You know my name,' I whispered.

'I learned of it. After we met, at your... "exhibition".'

The air-quotes around the word *exhibition* couldn't have been clearer. I blushed again. 'We were trying to find out who had stolen — er, taken the grimoire,' I said. 'It was important. I'm sorry for the deception. If we'd had any idea...' *that you were a real person and might actually show up, we'd never have been so damned crazy.*

Probably.

'Well, it succeeded,' she said, flashing me a small, surprising smile. A grin, even.

We, the bumbling Society, had amused the great and powerful Merlin.

Go, team.

'And much good may come of it,' she went on... sarcastically? Not?

Being Ves, I babbled. 'We... well, we found the grimoire, sure. Its current owner — or caretaker? — will be delighted to have it back. And we'll get the argent we need, for Torvaston's regulator. Orlando's working on it already, he's got the best in the industry helping him and finally we've held up our end. They can go ahead and build it. And if it works the way we're hoping it will, it could change everything. We're... we're bringing magick back.' Overwhelmed with sudden emotion, I could have cried. With relief, mostly, because I hadn't wanted to admit to myself how much fear I'd had. Fear that we would fail Orlando, the Society, magick — everything.

But I was babbling for another reason, too. A new, different flavour of fear.

You have changed, Cordelia Vesper. You know that you have, though you may not realise how much.

I had. She was right.

Let's not talk about that, my heart said. *Let's just talk about the mission. Nice, achievable goals, even if they were challenging. Measurable successes. Clear ways forward. Nobody needs to change in profound, irreversible ways, or become anything they aren't ready to be. I can just stay... Ves.*

But we don't get to choose who we become. Do we? We bumble from day to day, doing what we do, trying not to screw up; and inexorably we're swept along in whatever happens next. And then, and then, and then... you're someone you never thought you could be.

Maybe someone you never wanted to be.

'Is that the aim? Restoring magick?' said Merlin, setting down her pestle. Or mortar? Is the pestle the bowl bit, or the grinding tool?

Focus, Ves.

'It may sound crazy...' I began, and then couldn't think how to continue.

'Oh, no,' said Ophelia-Merlin. 'I should think it's achievable, with the right tools.'

Suddenly I didn't want to know what the right tools were. I couldn't have said why; I only felt a deep-seated feeling of panic. If I turned that corner, I knew I wouldn't be coming back.

'Do... you want to hear the story?' I croaked.

'Yes,' she said. 'Tell me everything.'

So I sat with Merlin the Master Magician and told her the whole story. And I mean, the *whole* story. More than I'd told the queen of Aylligranir. More than I'd told to anybody except Milady. Every. Single. Detail.

Which was basically me buckling under the pressure and prattling like an idiot again, but maybe I was usefully prattling. If anybody could help us push this insane project through, surely it was Merlin.

She asked a question or two here and there, but mostly she just let me talk. And when I'd finished explaining just why we were chasing down her grimoire, and the sequence of events that had led up to my presence in her fantastic Wizard's Lab; when at long last, I stopped burbling and fell silent; she sat staring at me with a tiny frown creasing her brow, and said nothing.

Folks, this is why I talk too much when I'm nervous. There is nothing — *nothing* — scarier than dead silence.

I cleared my throat. 'Anyway, I ought to be getting back to it. Mum and Jay will be wondering where I am, and we need to wrap things up with the Elvyngs. Get that argent back to Orlando. Go on with the mission.'

She said nothing.

'And I've taken up way too much of your time. I'm sure you're very busy.'

Making potions, apparently. What else did a living magickal legend get up to all day? I didn't bother asking. Chances of her giving me an answer seemed about nil.

I'd sunk onto a cushioned stool halfway through my narrative, when my still-wobbly legs began to give out on me. I now rose from it, with an air I hoped might pass for brisk, breezy and confident, and flashed her a professional smile. 'Thank you so much for your time, and of course for returning the grimoire. We really appreciate it.'

Turning to go, I realised I had no idea how to get out. I hadn't arrived here through anything so conventional as a door, so there was no point expecting to exit out of one. 'Would you be so kind...?' I said, waving my hands in a vanish-me-please gesture.

Her frown deepened, and creases appeared around her narrowed eyes. 'Yes,' she said.

But seconds passed and I wasn't vanished. Whatever she was saying yes to, it wasn't in response to my request.

I waited in stomach-churning discomfort.

'Yes, I think perhaps—' said Merlin (or Ophelia). Her eyes refocused on my face, and something blazed therein. Something magickal, about which I badly did not wish to think too hard. 'The signs are there,' she murmured.

I glanced around the room, but there was no one else in there. Just the two of us.

I cleared my throat again. 'Ma'am?' I said. 'Please let me go?'

She blinked. 'Ah,' she said, and waved a dismissive hand. 'I must consider the—'

Whatever it was she planned to consider must remain forever a mystery. With that careless wave of her hand, she cast me out of her wizardly grotto and back into what we mere ordinary mortals think of as reality.

15

I EMERGED BACK IN the Elvyngs' grimoire-cupboard, seated atop the glass case. Thankfully, the thing was made of sturdy stuff, for I didn't crash straight through it.

Being dizzy as hell and confused, I *did* promptly fall off it.

Sadly there was no Jay to catch me.

'Ouch,' I wheezed, picking myself up. 'Too much to hope for a nice, soft carpet—'

'Ves?' somebody yelled. 'Was that you?'

Jay appeared in the doorway, looking harassed.

'You mean the inelegant thud marking my undignified tumble off this delightful display case, and the ill-natured muttering with which I expressed my dissatisfaction?'

'Yeah, those.'

'Because who else could it possibly have been?'

'Exactly.'

I dusted myself off, rather crossly. 'Aren't you going to ask me where I've been?'

'Hadn't thought it necessary.'

'Because the story will naturally spill forth in my usual display of verbal diarrhoea?'

Jay just nodded, like, *obviously?*

I sighed. 'I went to Merlin's Secret Lab where I learned almost nothing, but at least the grimoire's back.' I peered through the clear glass. Yep, one priceless and elusive spell-book stashed therein. 'Great. Okay. Does Mr. Elvyng know? Can I call Crystobel?'

'Merlin's Secret Lab?'

'She's got a between-the-echoes thing. A bit like Baroness Tremayne's, but cooler.'

'How did you persuade her to return the grimoire?'

'I didn't. She borrowed the book one time, and would've returned it sooner, if she hadn't happened to forget for about a thousand years.'

'She... forgot.'

'She's absent-minded, but who isn't when you're wielding the ancient power of a lost age?'

Jay made his incredulous face.

'You didn't really think she was Merlin? I guess I didn't either. But she is. Also her name's Ophelia.' Jay clearly getting ready to voice a million questions of his own, I held up a hand. 'Don't ask me. She did not choose to tell me what any of that means.'

Jay digested that. 'And the other items?' he said.

'The what— oh, the other stolen things that Sally mentioned? No idea, but they probably ended up in the same place. Whether she borrowed those, too, or decided to keep them, I neither know nor care.'

Jay nodded, eyeing me with a slight frown. 'Are you okay?'

I ran my hands through my tumbled, jade-green hair, thus casting it into still greater disorder. 'I don't know. I feel as though I was just assessed for something, but I don't know what, and I don't feel good about it.'

'Pass or fail?'

What a very Jay question. 'No clue. Suspect pass, but could be either. And I'm frustrated that I didn't get any answers to anything else, either.'

'Well... mission accomplished, right?' said Jay, putting a hand under my elbow when I displayed a propensity to wobble. 'We have what we came for. We can move ahead.'

'True,' I said, with a deep sigh. 'True. Yay, we won.'

'Best detectives ever,' said Jay, with a small smile.

'Craziest detectives ever, and more dependent on deception, luck and outright fraud than any self-respecting detective is supposed to be. But hey, if it gets the job done.'

My own smile was rather humourless. I'd have to try harder.

Jay wasn't fooled. 'It'll be okay, Ves,' he said, giving my arm a friendly squeeze.

I turned troubled eyes on him, unable to feel comforted. 'Are you sure?'

'No, but... I have hope.'

'Care to share some of that hope juice? I seem to be fresh out.'

'By all means. We'll start with a cake or six, because you look like you could use the sugar. A barrel or two of wine. Bit of karaoke. And if you aren't feeling better by the end of all that, I'll eat my hat.'

'Which would be quite a sight, I grant you.' I straightened my spine, took a deep breath, and sallied forth. 'Onward to victory?'

'Onward to victory.'

I HAD THE SENSE to call Crystobel before our party-hard event, not after. She was pleased.

To say the least.

'You've what?' she said, after I'd dropped the news.

'Got your grimoire back. All sorted. It's at home with your father.'

'Really! Really?'

'Didn't you think we would?'

'I... hoped so, but everyone else we've consulted came up with nothing.'

I struggled with myself for a second, but decided to let it pass. If she had set us what she'd thought was an impossible mission in the full expectation that we would fail, well, too bad for her.

Never underestimate the power of a half-deranged Ves and her workaholic sidekick.

'Who took it?' she said, which was the question I'd been dreading. 'And how did they get in?'

Naturally, she needed that information. They'd want to shore up their security, make sure nobody could get a chance at swiping the grimoire again.

'Well,' I said slowly. 'This part gets a little improbable, if you'll bear with me.'

'All right...'

'Merlin took it. Or actually, she just borrowed it back for a bit, and forgot to return it. You should issue her with one hell of an overdue fee.'

If I was hoping the joke would help the dose go down easier, I was deluding myself. 'Merlin?' she said sharply. 'Actually Merlin? That's absurd.'

And I sighed.

I'd had a debate with Jay before I'd called. Me, I'd been in favour of concocting a more plausible version of events which didn't involve my having to conquer all of Crystobel's understandable incredulity and risk a verbal dismembering for being a filthy liar. Jay, of course, was in favour of telling the truth, the whole truth, and nothing but the impossible, ridiculous, who-the-hell-would-believe-me truth, gods damn it.

He won.

So I explained, again, and I was getting a bit tired of lengthy recountings-of-events followed by unlooked-for responses. Merlin had stared at me like she was seeing into the heart of the known universe, and said virtually nothing. Crystobel laughed in my face, only slowly came around to a place where she consented to take me seriously (sort of), and finally rang off in a bit of a huff.

The huff came about because I couldn't assure her that the grimoire wouldn't go missing again, or indeed that there was anything she could do about that either.

Really, if Merlin wanted a gateway in the Elvyng mansion so she could occasionally consult the grimoire, then the gateway was going to stay right where it was. Good luck talking her out of it.

I pointed out that Merlin could have just kept the grimoire forever, leaving the Elvyngs short both spell-book and its obscene purchase price, but Crystobel didn't take that well either.

'So I should be grateful for *mostly* retaining ownership over my own property?' she snapped.

That was the part where I gave up. If I ever saw Merlin again, I'd recommend her to go meet the Elvyngs and have a nice chat about her grimoire. Nothing short of that was going to convince Crystobel (for which I couldn't truly blame her).

'It's been great working with you, Crystobel,' I said. 'The Society will send a requisition for the argent soon, okay?'

Fortunately, her sense of professionalism won out over her discontent, and she didn't spit in my face down the phone. 'Of course,' she said. 'I'll have a shipment ready for you soon.'

Some gracious, mutual (and even vaguely sincere) praise followed, after which I hung up and awarded myself two minutes of deep breathing, with a side of daydreaming about cake and wine.

One last thing to do: call Val. She at least would be happy with us. The grimoire was real! No word of a lie! *This* of all mythical spell-books was the honest-to-gods truth!

But I was forgetting one small but crucial detail.

'That's fantastic Ves, and what did it say?' were her words upon hearing the news.

Oops.

'Er, no idea,' I admitted.

Ominous silence.

'I didn't get a chance to read it...'

'You didn't *read it*?'

'I was sort of distracted, and anyway the bit I saw wasn't comprehensible, I think it was in a script I don't know—'

'Tell me you at least took a picture?'

'I, uh, didn't have the chance, but before you kill me remember that Crystobel promised! *Promised,* Val. If you talk to her I'm sure she will arrange to get you a look at it.'

'Let's all hope so,' she said dangerously, and then she hung up.

And that's when Jay and I decided we *really* needed that drink.

WORD OF WARNING FOR YOU.

Never challenge Jay to a karaoke contest.

Really, I should've known. The man's part Yllanfalen, and I've had every possible clue as to the musical genius he's hiding under those flashy Waymastery skills.

But I'd had some of that wine he mentioned, and I wasn't thinking clearly by then.

'Jay,' I'd said, after he'd favoured us all with a few of my favourite eighties rock anthems. 'What are you doing with the Society? I mean, what are you even doing? You should be a rock star.'

He was pleased, I could tell. But being Jay, he was also effortlessly cool. 'I don't want to be a rock star,' he said. 'I want to be the Society Waymaster, and your sidekick, and maybe do a little music magick on the side. Shall we go Home?'

'I want to sing again,' I'd thought it wise to declare, and gods help me, I did.

Sometime later, when I'd finished my Mary Bennet routine and consented to be coaxed out the door, I found myself halfway back Home on foot. Barefoot, if you please, and don't ask me where my sandals went because I haven't a clue. The silver moon shone brightly upon the quiet country lane along which Jay and I tottered, not quite at the point where we were obliged to prop each other up, but definitely the worse for wear.

'Your sister's great,' I was saying. 'What a talent.'

'Which one?'

'Right. Indira, I meant. She's amazing. You're amazing. Is your whole family like that?'

'Depends who you ask. My parents would say yes.'

'What about you?'

'Modesty's considered socially acceptable, Ves.'

'All right. Excepting yourself, is your whole family like that?'

'Yes.'

'See, that's what I thought.' I fell into a short episode of brooding. 'I wish I'd had a sibling,' I announced. 'A sister. I'd have liked that. Hey, maybe she would've been amazing, too.'

'Not a doubt of it,' said Jay.

'Maybe I *do* have a sister,' I said, struck by a sudden flash of inspiration. 'My Dad could have hundreds of kids, for all I know.'

'He could certainly have one or two more,' Jay allowed. 'Have you asked him?'

I vigorously shook my head. 'But I don't think Indira and I can ever be friends,' I said.

'Why not? She likes you.'

'I like her, too!' I said earnestly. 'Only, she doesn't like Phil Collins.'

'It's a failing I've often had to speak to her about.'

I nodded sadly. I'd sung three of his greatest hits only an hour or so earlier, or perhaps I should say I'd mangled them. Poor, wonderful songs, they deserved better than me.

'You'll have to change her mind,' Jay persevered. 'Invite her to a music party.'

'*Not* a karaoke party.'

He laughed. 'You were pretty good, honestly.'

I gave him the side-eye.

He grinned. 'No, really.'

I put my nose in the air. 'I may not be a natural pop singer, but Addie loves me.'

'That she does.'

'Do *you* have a unicorn Familiar?'

'Nope.'

'There,' I said, unsure what point it was I thought I had won, but certain of having triumphed at *something*.

'There's Home,' Jay said, pointing. And indeed, upon the silver-lit horizon of harvest-ready wheat there appeared our beloved House, only the top of the roof visible yet, for we were toiling slowly up a woldy slope.

'Blessed Home,' I murmured, delighted to see it. Then, a thought filtered slowly into my wine-fogged brain. 'Wait. Why is it visible?'

Jay glanced sharply at me. 'What?'

'My first time here, I got lost for days looking for it. Because it isn't visible from this distance.'

Jay frowned. He, of course, hadn't had much occasion to wander up to the House on foot like this.

'How did you find it on your first day?' I asked.

'Way-henge.'

'Seriously?'

He nodded. 'Milady marked it on my app for me.'

If we'd had apps like that a decade ago when I was first rolling up to the Society, things might've been different. I certainly wouldn't have been lost for half of eternity.

But if they had, I might never have met Addie.

'Come to think of it, though, you're right,' said Jay. 'I don't usually see it until I'm much closer.'

I looked all around, and behind me, as though something to explain House's unusual visibility choices might materialise out of the darkness. 'Do you think we should hurry?' I suggested.

'You think there might be something wrong?'

'Wrong? I don't know. But *something*? Definitely.'

Jay took my arm. 'Well then, let's get a move on.'

16

We trotted up House's driveway, passing in between those ancient oaks all silver-painted by the moon. Upon discovering the front door sitting open at three in the morning, we entered the building at a near run.

'House,' I said, a bit breathless. 'Is everything all right?'

I couldn't see much. The door might be open but no lights illuminated the entrance hall. That air of dead-of-night stillness shrouded everything, as indeed it was supposed to at that hour, and though Jay and I stood for a couple of minutes, we heard nothing but silence.

'House?' I said again. I found the nearest wall and laid a hand against it. Cool, smooth brick met my fingers, and that was all. Nothing untoward.

'Seems normal enough,' I whispered, and that's when the lights came on.

'Aha,' said Merlin, coming into the hall through a far doorway, her arms full of boxes. 'I've brought your argent.'

I blinked stupidly at her. 'What?'

'Your argent,' she repeated, and offered the stack of boxes to me. They were ordinary parcel boxes, though I could feel the strength of their warding enchantments even from several feet away. The cardboard hid some of the Elvyngs' patented safe boxes, I guessed, and inside those...

'Wait,' I said, looking wildly about. 'How is it that *you* have the argent? And — and how are you *here*?'

Her brows rose, and she looked more closely at me than she had yet. 'Oh,' she said, no doubt observing my inebriated state. Fortunately, her expression was more amused than disapproving.

'You haven't done something to the House?' I said, unable to suppress a flicker of panic. The visibility, the open door — it wasn't normal and it wasn't right.

'No, no,' she said. 'The House has been very welcoming.'

I relaxed a little. House was very, very hard to find, when it wanted to be. If it didn't want Merlin in here, she'd never have discovered its whereabouts.

Probably.

Was Merlin powerful enough to outwit our House?

'If House didn't want her here, we'd be seeing some sign of it,' Jay murmured to me, *sotto voce.*

And he had a point. If she had forced her way in here, House wouldn't be doing all this nothing about it.

'It was visible,' I said to Merlin, attempting to explain. 'From the fields, way back there.' I waved an arm.

'I did ask it for your whereabouts,' she said. 'Having gathered that you were absent, I requested its assistance in bringing you Home. Perhaps that is why it rendered itself perceptible from an unusual distance.'

A nearby floating lamp flickered briefly, and I felt a sense of warmth. Approval from House.

'Right,' I said, relaxing. 'Sorry. Um, hi! Lovely to see you again.'

'Perhaps I can take those,' said Jay, stepping forward.

'You must be Jay,' said Merlin, handing off the stack of boxes to him. 'Excellent.'

'Is it?' said he, hefting the load as though the boxes weighed nothing. Hopefully they didn't literally weigh nothing. Just a handy enchantment to take the burden out of carting them around... right?

'I was hoping to meet you both,' said Merlin. 'It is important that Ves should have suitable support, at least for the early years.'

'Support?' I felt that lurking sense of dread again, the same as had plagued me during my last conversation with this woman. 'For what? The early years of what?'

'If we may find somewhere suitable to talk?'

'Milady's tower,' I said promptly. Whatever it was this woman proposed to say to me, or to do to me, I wanted Milady to be present for it.

'An excellent choice,' she said.

I exchanged a puzzled look with Jay, who glanced at the boxes he carried. 'I guess these can come with us for now,' he said. 'I can take them to Orlando in the morning.'

Few places at Home could be more secure than Milady's tower, so I made no objection. As we clambered our way up the stairs, more questions flooded into my befuddled brain.

'Ophelia,' I said. 'Or Merlin. Sorry to be inquisitive, but how *do* you come to have Crystobel's argent?'

'I thought it polite to pay a call on her,' she said, sounding for all the world like an eighteenth century society lady. 'Having inconvenienced her and her father over the matter of the grimoire, of course.' Something in her tone hinted at a hidden layer of steel. Had it been a mere social call, or had she also wanted to inspect those who had access to the magick contained within the grimoire? I was suddenly grateful that I wasn't standing in Crystobel Elvyng's shoes just now. Had the uses to which they'd put the grimoire's enchantments satisfied Merlin?

'And when,' Ophelia/Merlin continued, 'I understood she intended an immediate dispatch of your argent, I offered to convey it.'

'How kind,' I murmured. 'But, um, you aren't here just to deliver the silver?'

'Indeed not.'

I rubbed at my face, tripped over the next step, and wished to all the gods we hadn't chosen this of all possible nights to let our proverbial hair down. My wine-fogged brain refused to keep up with these strings of surprising events. I felt half asleep and half awake, dreaming yet not.

'Perhaps I might be of assistance?' said Merlin/Ophelia, and without waiting for an answer, she touched my elbow. The lightest of touches, there and then gone, but in an instant my inebriation vanished.

I straightened, blinking. 'That is a *good* trick,' I said, with a certain amount of envy. 'Thank you. Could you do Jay, as well?'

'*Do* what to me?' said Jay incredulously, but in another instant Merlin had performed her excellent drink-busting charm upon him as well, and he followed that up with an enthralled, '*Oh.*' He added, 'That's way better than Anaya's!'

Dimly, I recalled that this was the name of yet another of Jay's sisters.

'It is one of the inherited arts,' murmured Merlin, striding slowly up the stairs beside me, and without exhibiting the smallest signs of tiring, despite her apparent age. 'Not among the most useful or the most spectacular, of course, but it has its uses.'

'A.. Merlin-inherited art?' I hazarded.

She nodded.

I travelled up the rest of the stairs in silence, trying unsuccessfully to parse that unlikely piece of information. Something about her Merlinness involved inherited charms, presumably those ancient magicks my mother had spoken of. And one of them was... an inebriation-busting charm.

Right.

At last we reached the top of the many flights of stairs, and arrived at Milady's tower-top room. The oaken door, of course, was closed.

I knocked. 'Erm, Milady? Sorry to bother you at this hour, but it's quite important.'

'Come in,' she said instantly.

'Sorry,' I said again, upon entering the room. My bare feet, slightly damaged from the walk, relished the sensation of soft, thick carpet under my toes. 'I know it's an unsociable time, but...' I stopped talking, because the wall-lamps were softly aglow, a set of three deep armchairs sat arranged around a low, pearl-inlaid coffee table I hadn't seen before, and a tea set sat ready, with several elegant porcelain cups and two pots. One for tea, one for chocolate, judging from the aromas.

We hadn't taken Milady by surprise. It might be three in the morning, but she was waiting for us.

'This looks nice,' I said lamely, claiming one of the chairs.

'Welcome Ves, Jay,' said Milady. 'And Merlin. It's an honour to have you with us again.'

Again? Jay and I shared a *what-in-the-name-of* look.

'One of my predecessors, I fancy,' said Merlin, taking her seat.

'I had thought the role lapsed,' said Milady. 'Long ago.'

'I have considered it advisable to remain hidden,' said Merlin.

None of this made much sense to me, or to Jay, either. We sat in shared silence, thoughts awhirl.

'Is it time?' said Milady.

'Not immediately. But the time approaches, and it would be well to prepare.'

At which point, she looked at me.

I didn't like that look either, nor the timing. I avoided it by lunging for the coffee table, and divesting it of one cup of chocolate. This I attempted to sip in elegant fashion, and ended up gulping half of it down in two swallows.

My hands were shaking.

Jay, sensibly appointing himself spokesperson, said: 'May I ask what's afoot?'

Milady said nothing, leaving Merlin the floor.

Merlin — or Ophelia — shifted in her seat, betraying a trace of discomfort at last. 'You understand the nature of the Merlin role, of course?'

'We never heard it referred to as a *role* until two minutes ago,' said Jay.

'In other words, no,' I croaked.

'Many years ago,' she answered. 'Many *centuries* ago, the man remembered as Merlin wrought magicks of un-fathomable power across the British Isles. He was, and is, among the greatest of magickal legends these shores have ever produced. All this is known.

'What is not known is what became of him when he died. He had no wish to permit his extraordinary powers to die away with him. Perhaps it was arrogance; perhaps it was foresight. He may have seen that we would need those powers, someday far in the future.

'So he chose a successor. An apprentice, if you will, but one who inherited the greater part of Merlin's powers upon his death, as well as much of his knowledge. And he charged his apprentice to do the same, whenever his own time should come. By no means should Merlin's magick ever be permitted to fade away.'

'You're wielding fifteen-hundred year old magick?' I squeaked. My brain stuttered and died just trying to pic-ture the kind of potency she was talking about.

'Some of it has been lost to time, of course,' she said, nodding at me. 'Merlin's magick is a degree lessened each time it is passed to a new host, and some of the things he knew are no longer remembered now. But what remains of it is still considerable.'

'Interesting,' I said.

Interesting indeed. When Ophelia said *considerable,* she meant *of unimaginable depth compared to weak and faded modern magick.* Yes, she was just one person, but still. The *possibilities.*

'And in my turn, I shall need someone to carry these powers into the future,' Ophelia continued briskly. 'Someone who will put them to good use.'

She was looking steadily at me as she uttered most of this. I have no idea what my face was doing, but my brain repeated just the one word, over and over: *no, no no no no no no...*

Milady said, 'Someone dedicated to protecting and preserving magick, perhaps.'

'And restoring it for the future,' said Jay, the traitor.

'Wait,' I said, breathless. 'It — you — surely you can't mean *me.*'

'You have shown a remarkable capacity to absorb unusual and potent magick,' said Merlin. 'You also possess a kinship with creatures such as the unicorn, and an affinity with ancient magicks most can in no way fathom, such as the Lyre of the Yllanfalen. And your morals, your priorities, are exactly where they ought to be.'

'You also have the full support of the Society,' said Milady.

'And your friends,' said Jay quietly. I shot a sharp look at him. How could he be so laid back about this? Why wasn't he freaking out, like I was?

'This is—' I groped for a fitting word. 'Insane. Impossible. You can't be serious. Jay, tell me you don't *believe* this craziness?'

Jay's smile was a little strained. 'Too crazy, even for Ves?'

'*Way* too crazy!'

'We've little reason not to believe it,' he said. 'And imagine what it would be like, to have powers like this at the Society's disposal. We need this, Ves.'

'I don't,' I said vehemently. 'I can't do this. Ophelia, you've got the wrong person. I haven't been the same since Vale — the damned lyre — it almost tore me apart.'

'But it did not,' said Merlin.

'It might yet,' I muttered darkly.

Merlin shook her head. 'The worst is in the past.'

'Until you dump an ocean of ancient magick on my head. *Then* I fly to pieces.'

'I do not think you will,' she said, damnably serene.

'I have full confidence in you, Ves,' said Milady. 'This comes as no surprise to me.'

'I realise this is a great deal to take in,' Merlin said, inadequately.

'*You*, perhaps, do,' I said. 'But can you tell me you've never regretted the day you agreed to take on this role?' I was thinking of the life she seemed to lead, tucked away from the world among the echoes of a distant past. Safely hidden. Completely alone.

'Sometimes,' she said. 'But the things I have been able to achieve—'

'I have to go,' I blurted, and shot out of my chair. 'Sorry, I... I have to go.' I was out of the door and halfway down the stairs in seconds, running hard. Running away. I ran and ran, clattering back down all those long flights of stairs, through corridor after twisting corridor, doors that opened for me before I ever had a chance to touch them.

I ended at last somewhere I'd scarcely ever been before.

The parlour at the heart of Home. House's favourite room.

'House,' I panted, collapsing into one of the delicately upholstered mahogany chairs. 'Shut the door. Please, don't open it to anybody else. Not yet.'

The door creaked slowly shut behind me, locked with a reassuring snap, and I was safe. Safe from importuning Merlins, encouraging Miladies, or supportive Jays.

A fire flickered into being in the grate, and roared into comforting life. Better still, the opposite wall buckled, and a narrow bed slithered free of it, thickly covered in a floral duvet and drowning in pillows.

'Thank you,' I said weakly, trying unsuccessfully to stem a confusing and rather humiliating flow of tears. But the bed was welcoming, and as I collapsed face-first onto it, I watered the pillows pretty liberally. I'm not proud of it, but I'm here to tell you the truth.

Sometime much later, I fell into an exhausted sleep.

17

SHOCK IS A STRANGE experience. Events that are (arguably) positive, amazing and overall pretty great can be as much of a shock to the system as more unpleasant happenings. Who knew?

I say arguably positive, because I was by no means sold on the whole Merlin deal.

Why don't we do pros and cons?

Pro number one: *Power.* Who isn't just a little bit seduced by that, at one point or another? I've never been power hungry, but I couldn't altogether resist the allure of that much magick at my disposal. That much arcane knowledge. All the things I could *do...* Jay was right. We could use it.

Pro number two: Respect. To be Merlin, *the* Merlin, would be to join the magickal insider club for real. And for good. No one would argue with my right to do, or know, pretty much anything I wanted. Plus, I'd get to hobnob with all the magickal greats. Surely? Ophelia might have chosen to hide, but that didn't mean I would have to... right?

Pro number three: Long life, sort of. Was Ophelia any older than the average human woman, or was it merely that she'd skipped a lot of years? Either way, I might get to see what the world looks like in a century.

Con number one: Long life. If I am still kicking around in a century, then everyone I know and love today will be dead. Not for nothing was I struck by the loneliness of Ophelia's existence.

Con number two: Power, and indeed respect. Look at that train of thought. I could do whatever I like! No one could argue with me! That, my friends, is the high road to Hell.

More cons: I'm truly not sure that I could handle that much magick. I wasn't kidding when I said it might break me. Without Addie, I'd already be a gibbering wreck. What would Merlin's powers do to me?

The only way to find out the answer to that little conundrum? Try it and see! And hope I don't explode.

I know this has been my favoured *modus operandi* for some time now, but never with these kinds of stakes.

I, reckless Ves, am running scared. How's that for an about-face?

Not that there has been much actual running involved. I've been holed up in House's favourite room for a night and most of a day, and I can't tell you that I feel any more inclined to emerge. I don't want to face Milady, who spoke of my incipient Merlinhood as though it would be a lovely little promotion, no big deal. I don't want to run the risk that our current Merlin herself will still be out there, waiting to coolly tell me more about how ideal I am for this doom.

I don't want to face Jay, who accepted both Merlin's existence and her mad proposition without a blink, and smilingly told me to go for it.

If anyone's taught sceptical Jay to accept pure craziness at face value, it's undoubtedly me, but that isn't a reflection to make me feel any better right now.

To hell with it.

'House,' I said at one point. 'How did this happen? I mean, how did I get here? I never wanted anything this big. Truly, I didn't. I've just been doing my job.'

And later, 'Okay, I developed a few gigantic dreams here and there, but they weren't for me. They were for magick as a whole. I'm not legend material. Am I?'

Dear House let me ramble in peace. I wasn't really expecting a response, of course. Just talking to the wall.

Sometimes it helps a person achieve some measure of clarity.

Sometimes.

House did keep me well supplied, though. Three meals a day, served on the dot of eight o'clock, one o'clock and seven o'clock. Afternoon tea at three. An en suite bathroom just off the parlour, which I strongly suspect was not there before. A comfortably blazing fire, which may seem odd for the end of summer, but the parlour's oddly chilly.

I studied the portraits on the walls at my leisure, without deriving any further clues as to the probable identities of the subjects. Or indeed, who had put them there. Were they the property of Milady, or had House preserved them for reasons of its own?

I did ask, but nobody answered.

'One thing that interests me,' I said, shortly after dinner (pancakes, of course. How well House knows me). 'If there's one hereditary magickal role derived from an ancient legend, are there more? If Merlin was, and is, real, how about Morgan le Fay? Circe? Hell, how about Gandalf?'

'I knew you would ask those questions, sooner or later,' came Milady's voice.

After a solid day of silence, save only for my own voice, I near jumped out of my skin.

I may have sworn a bit.

'Sorry,' I said immediately. 'I was startled.'

'I do apologise. I could not think of a way to announce myself.'

'Have you been here the whole time?' I asked.

'No. But occasionally I've looked in on you.'

I suppose if I'd wanted absolute peace and privacy, hiding in the heart of the House was not the best choice.

'Jay is most concerned,' added Milady.

'Sorry,' I said weakly, afflicted with a sudden rush of guilt. Poor Jay. I'd left him kicking his heels all day, and apparently he was kind enough to worry about me.

I checked my phone, but he hadn't messaged or called. He'd been giving me space.

That, or my phone wouldn't work in House's favourite room. It did have a certain seventeenth-century air about it, after all.

'Are you perhaps ready to emerge?' said Milady. 'Merlin has left us for the present.'

'I suppose I must,' I sighed. 'It's childish to hide from my problems, isn't it? As though if they can't see me, they'll go away.'

'It is natural enough, at times of great stress. I myself once spent two days complete in this very room, quite alone.'

'Really?' I sat up a bit. 'Why did you do that?'

She hesitated long enough that I wasn't sure she would answer. But then she said, 'I had been offered the role I now occupy, and I did not know whether or not to accept.'

'Wow. Offered by whom?'

She chuckled. 'I cannot provide too many details, of course. Not at this time.'

At this time. That meant: not now, but maybe someday.

'I need hardly ask whether or not you regretted it,' I said.

'For the most part, I have not. I have been able to achieve far more than I ever dreamed possible, and it is worthy work.'

Worthy work. Yes. What these kinds of choices came down to, in essence, was: were we willing to devote everything we had to our work, at any price?

And I suppose I was frightened because I already knew the answer to that question. I'd been saying yes for years.

I would say yes again.

I just didn't know whether I was up to the cost.

My hands were shaking again, so I clasped them tightly together and tried to appear unconcerned.

But the shaking spread to my whole body, and when my teeth began to chatter I gave up on trying to hide it. 'I don't know if I can do it,' I said. 'I really don't know.'

'We never know what we can do,' said Milady gently. 'We never feel ready. All you can do, dear Ves, is decide whether you're willing to try.'

Giddy gods. I gritted my teeth on a rising tide of nausea.

'If it helps, I have complete confidence in you,' Milady continued. 'So does your excellent friend Jay. So does Val; indeed, I have no doubt that the entire Society would support you without question. To us, the question is not *can she do it,* but *what will she achieve when she does*?'

'I appreciate that,' I said tightly. 'Really, I do. But I'm also seeing the dark side. Like, how many people are going to be disappointed when I burst like rotten fruit?'

'Ves...'

'Though if that happens I'll be a goner, so I suppose I won't care anyway.'

'I am one hundred percent positive it will not kill you.'

'Really? That certain?'

'To partially answer your earlier question: yes, there are other such roles in this world. Or, there have been; I am not sure myself how many yet survive, or who now embodies each archetype. But I have never heard of anyone's dying in the attempt of it.'

A flicker of excitement rose, somewhere in my beleaguered soul. 'Who are the other ones?'

'Some of your guesses were rather shrewd.'

'Gandalf wasn't one of the shrewd ones?'

'Not that one, no.'

'Curse it.' I'd been hoping for Gandalf. 'But Morgan le Fay? And Circe?'

'Again, I do not know if either of those still walk these worlds. But they are certainly past archetypes, and may still be current.'

'I bet Merlin knows.'

'I imagine she might, yes.'

And my traitorous curiosity betrayed me.

All the things Merlin knows.

All the things I would know, if I became the next Merlin-archetype.

'Sideline,' I said. 'All those three names are from ancient times. Are there *new* archetypes? I mean, has anybody from a more recent era become such a legend as to qualify?'

Her silence was... eloquent.

'I cannot discuss that,' she finally said.

Milady being cagey meant... I'd stumbled over something.

'You're one of them,' I gasped. 'A newly minted archetype. Or an old one?'

'Ves, these are things I cannot discuss.'

'I respect your right to conceal anything you choose, of course, but... why can't you?'

'For the same reasons Merlin has chosen to hide herself. Morgan and Circe may be doing the same. Legends loom especially large in this modern world, Ves, and that has its drawbacks as well as its advantages. Anonymity grants me a degree of safety and freedom that I might not otherwise enjoy.'

'I think I understand.'

'I am sorry for it, sometimes. Secrecy has its costs as well.'

I thought of Ophelia/Merlin's lonely abode, and nodded.

'Well,' I said briskly, and hauled myself out of my comfortable chair. 'It's time I stopped bemoaning my fate and got on with it.'

'I have always admired your courage, Ves,' said Milady quietly. 'I realise this is not easy for you.'

I bowed my acknowledgement of this vote of confidence. 'Where might I find Jay?'

'He's in the library, with Valerie.'

'Right.' I made it halfway to the door before I was halted by an appalling thought. 'Wait. These archetypes. Nicolas Flamel... he isn't one of them, is he?' The words I'd scrawled in my notebook not long ago floated behind my eyes. *Nicolas Flamel sucks.*

Milady laughed. 'To my knowledge, he is not.'

'Thank goodness for that.'

18

I MADE MY WAY to the library with some feelings of mild apprehension. Jay might justifiably kill me for having left him to fret all day. Val might justifiably murder me for having failed to get her the contents of Merlin's grimoire.

My life was in all kinds of danger, lately.

I found Jay sitting in one of the deep, silver-brocaded chairs before the hearth in the main hall of the library. Those self-same chairs I hardly saw anyone use, until recently when Val sat there with Crystobel Elvyng.

Now Jay sat alone, a book on his lap but his gaze fixed upon the empty grate. He didn't look worried so much as forlorn, which tore at my heart-strings rather a lot.

'For a man pretending to read, you're doing an abominable job,' I said.

He looked up sharply, and then sat up, so fast he almost tossed his book onto the floor. 'Ves! You're okay. I mean… are you okay?'

I wondered, too late, what I looked like. I hadn't bothered to check, and considering my frame of mind, I probably looked like a washed-out wreck. 'I'm fine,' I said, attempting a reassuring smile. 'And I'm really sorry that I worried you. I should have thought of that before.'

Jay smiled. 'In your shoes, I'm not sure I would have reacted much differently,' he said, generous as always. 'It's a big ask.'

Daringly, I took the opposite seat to Jay's. It felt like I was lounging all over hallowed ground, and I half expected Val to come shooting in from her desk, ready to incinerate me on the spot.

But she didn't, and nothing happened, so I relaxed a bit. 'It's just been a… strange couple of months,' I said, with towering understatement. 'I don't feel much like myself anymore.' I remembered Rob's recent words, and his encouragement to visit Grace for some in-house counselling. I'd spurned the very idea at the time, but.

Perhaps he had a point.

'I think you *aren't* like your old self,' Jay said. 'You aren't quite the person you were when I first met you.'

Dismal thought.

'But is that a bad thing?' he went on. 'You were magnificent before. Now you're going to be epic.'

I had to grin. 'Epic! Will people pen long accounts of my daring exploits?'

'Undoubtedly. Great tomes of extravagant praise.'

My smile faded. 'But no, because in this new future scenario, I wouldn't be me anymore. I'd be doing the things I do under the banner of Merlin's legacy. Who will remember Ves?'

Jay looked long at me. 'Is that what's bothering you?'

I thought about it. 'Not the likelihood of not being personally remembered. That is the fate that awaits almost all of us. But ceasing to be me anymore, in my own lifetime? Yes, that bothers me. What's left of Ophelia? What became of her life?'

'You can do this your own way, Ves. Like you do everything. You don't have to let Ophelia's choices rule you.'

'But maybe she made them because she had to.'

'Maybe she didn't. Maybe she made those choices because she wanted to.'

I shifted in my seat. 'I need to talk to her again. I mean, I don't even know why she wants to replace herself, or what I'd be expected to do as the next Merlin.'

Jay nodded. 'She anticipated that, so she left me the means to reach her.'

'She left *you* the means?'

'She's got a little henge, apparently. I assume it's attached to that secret abode you visited. If you're ready to talk, I can take you there.'

I felt a surge of gut-gnawing apprehension, and badly wanted to say no.

But fear is there to stop us from doing things. That is its sole purpose. And while, on occasion, it's wise to pay attention, most of the time it's talking crap.

'Right,' I said. 'If you're at leisure now, shall we get it over with?'

Jay smiled like he was impressed with me, which made me feel a tiny bit better. If Jay experiences such ordinary human sensations as nerves or indeed screaming terror, I've rarely caught a glimpse of it, but I suppose he must. 'I can take you right now,' he said, and stood up.

'Ves?'

I looked up. Val came floating towards us in her spectacularly green Elvyng chair, one hand held out to Jay. He placed into it the book he'd been ignoring, and she settled it tenderly in her lap. 'You're going?' she said.

I nodded.

'Good.' She looked piercingly at me, and added, 'You've got this, Ves.'

'And there I thought I was doing a good job of exuding an effortless calm.'

Val snorted. Then, pointing a finger at me, she said: 'Get me that grimoire.'

Before I could reply, she'd turned her chair and sailed back into the depths of her beloved library.

WHEN JAY WHIRLED US away upon the Winds, we emerged into a compact little grove, ringed around with rowan and ash trees, and carpeted in deep moss and clover. Merlin's henge was a collection of low, time-worn stones, reddish-brown in hue and veined in moss agate.

At one edge of the grove rose a low-roofed cottage, timber-beamed, with whitewashed walls and a thatched roof. For a building that apparently dated from somewhere in the late fourteen hundreds, it looked curiously new and fresh. This couldn't be the dwelling of the original Merlin; it wasn't old enough. But its state of preservation owed much to the powerful enchantments that kept this place just a little separated from the regular flow of time. Which long-forgotten Merlin had created this place?

I set off in the direction of the cottage, heading for the diminutive, blue-painted front door that led into it.

Halfway there, I realised Jay was not following.

When I turned, I saw he'd settled himself cross-legged in the middle of the henge, and looked fixed there for a while.

'Aren't you coming?' I called.

He shook his head. 'Not my place.'

'Not your place? Jay, you've every right to be a part of this.'

His smile was faint. 'I don't think so. I'd be intruding.'

I went back over to him, and held out my hand. 'If you mean you'd rather not be dragged into this, I can understand and respect that. But we're friends, and we're partners, and if I'm given the choice I don't want to do this without you.'

Jay still looked doubtful.

'If it's Merlin you're worried about, I think she acknowledged and accepted your involvement when she left the means to bring me here with you.'

'Instead of one of the several other Waymasters at Home?'

'Jay, don't be an idiot. She could've just opened a gateway. You know, like she did at the Elvyng house.'

His eyebrows shot up. 'I... didn't think of that.'

I grinned, and wiggled my outstretched fingers. 'Come on. Somebody's got to keep me from doing anything too completely crazy.'

'Since when have I ever had that power?' said Jay, not without justice. But he permitted me to pull him to his feet, and when I set off again for Merlin's cottage he came with me.

'Ves,' said Ophelia shortly afterwards, as she answered the door. 'Excellent. Do, please, come in, both of you.'

Feeling obscurely pleased to be addressed as *Ves,* rather than anything more intimidatingly formal, I followed her inside.

I soon concluded that some kind of illusion was going on somewhere, for there were more rooms inside than seemed possible. Ophelia led us through a small kitchen (not without its modern conveniences); a cosy parlour, resplendent with polished wood and tapestry; a book-room stuffed with volumes both aged and new; and finally back into the workroom I'd seen before, which was far too big for the cottage's confines.

'This,' she said as we entered, 'is inherited from the first Merlin, or so it's said. The rest of the building has been added at different, later times.'

'Has every Merlin lived here?' I ventured. Subtext: would I be living here, too, someday?

'I assume so,' said Ophelia. 'I lived here with my predecessor for some years before he moved on.'

Moved on. I hesitated, but I had to ask. 'Do you mean... did he die, or...?'

She shook her head, busying herself with a brisk tidying-up of the cluttered chamber. 'Not then. He spoke of a desire to travel beyond the borders of Britain. I do not know where he was, when he finally died.'

Heartened by this vision of life after Merlinhood, I perched atop my chosen stool from before. Jay had taken a similar seat, and looked similarly uncertain. But when I looked at him, he managed to find for me an encouraging smile.

Poor Jay. Remorse smote me again. From the moment he'd joined the Society, he had been swept up in my orbit, and I had no doubt I had run him ragged since. I hadn't meant to, but did that matter?

I needed to think of a way to make it up to him. Or at the least, to show the enormous gratitude I felt for his staunch presence at my side, no matter how crazy I got, or how foolishly I'd failed to listen to him.

'You'll have questions?' said Ophelia into the silence.

'Right. Yes,' I said, dragging back my wandering thoughts. 'I was wondering... about the practicalities, I suppose. Like, how does it work? Will I be your apprentice? Will I live here? How is the role handed over? What will I do, as Merlin? And... and what won't I do, anymore?'

She nodded along with each question, and when my trail of worries had come to a close, she spoke with the kind of brisk efficiency which made short work of my anxieties.

'You will be my apprentice for a time, though you won't have to live here if you would prefer not to. I can arrange for a gateway to be available for your use. You won't have to give up your present occupation, if that concerns you. In fact, I would rather that you did not. It is my hope that Merlin's legacy will be used to support your stated goal of a magickal restoration for Britain, and indeed beyond, and you will best achieve that by remaining with the Society.' She took a breath. 'There is no complicated process in handing over the role. It will not hurt you.'

Which neatly answered most of my questions, and quieted some of my fears. I wouldn't have to change completely. I could still be me, and do the things I do. Hopefully.

But.

'If you'll forgive me for prying,' I said. 'Why is it that you want to hand off the role? Are you not... happy with it?' For while she was no longer a young woman, she wasn't a crone either. She had nothing of the look of a woman in imminent danger of her life, nor of a woman in urgent need of retirement. If it wasn't those things that spurred her to seek a replacement, what was it? Something about the role itself?

Ophelia met my eyes, briefly, and looked away. 'I have not been a stellar Merlin,' she said quietly. 'I have tried my best, but... the things at which I have excelled have done little to further the role. I have compiled a new grimoire. I have developed new enchantments, new magicks, derived from all those ancient practices I have inherited. But I have not used them. It has been my nature to remain within these walls, working alone. Is that what Merlin should be? Is that why his powers have been handed down? I think not.' She shook her head, and I saw raw regret in her face. 'For three years, I have been searching for someone who could carry those powers back into the real world. Someone who will use them, who will do something that matters. Someone who will not be alone; someone with the right people beside her.' Her glance acknowledged Jay, and her words encompassed the Society as a whole. 'I think I have found that person at last,' she said, looking squarely at me again. 'I am well aware of the trepidation you must feel, but I assure you I will do everything in my power to make the process as painless for you as possible.'

There was an undercurrent of pleading in her words, I realised. She really, badly wanted someone to say yes.

She wanted *me* to say yes.

I swallowed another surge of terror, and said: 'Must it be me? Are you *sure*?'

'Who can ever be absolutely sure of anything?' she countered. 'But as far as I can judge, I believe you to be the right candidate.'

'But... why?'

She'd already answered that question, of course. Something to do with my capacity to absorb magick, my affinity with ancient musical wonders and mythical creatures — none of which I could understand or explain. I struggled to believe it. I struggled to feel that these happenstances were anything I could claim, anything I could take credit for. They were just... me.

Ophelia's eyebrows twitched. Amusement? 'Humility is healthy,' she said. 'But look back over your track record these several years past, and tell me I am asking the wrong person.'

'Touché,' I sighed. I could bleat a bit more, if I wanted to. I could bang on about my lack of inherent magickal prowess — I wasn't a natural genius like Jay or Indira, and I lacked the discipline to study and learn as much as someone like them. Or Val. But those things weren't really being called for, were they? If she needed someone with a cause, and a support network, and just enough reckless determination to tackle utterly stupid goals in the name of magick, well... that's exactly what a Ves is for. Right?

'Okay then,' I said, all in a rush. 'I accept.'

There. I'd said it, and that was a promise. I couldn't turn chicken and back out now.

Ophelia smiled, the first real smile I had seen from her. It had a great deal of relief in it. 'And you?' she said, turning to Jay. 'Are you in agreement?'

Jay looked rather wide-eyed, and I could picture the words scrolling through his brain. *Just exactly what am I agreeing to do here?* But to his credit, with only a visible swallow, he said: 'Absolutely.'

'I don't suppose you'd make a Merlin of Jay instead?' I offered. 'He's much more responsible than me, and cleverer, and he's more powerful, too. He's used to wielding magick of absurd potency. He'd be great!'

Jay's eyebrows had climbed into his hair at this portrait of himself, and his eyes telegraphed a frantic *no, thank you,* at me.

Fortunately for us both, Ophelia shook her head. 'I have alternative ideas in mind for Jay Patel,' she said, and if those words terrified Jay half as much as they did me, then we were going to need another karaoke night in pretty short order.

19

Two days later, and I had my gateway straight into the heart of Merlin's grove all set up. Ophelia had constructed one for me in my own room, with a silver-shimmering pentagram drawn onto the floor by her own hand.

'Oooh,' I'd said, enthralled. 'What does the star do?'

'Shows you where it is,' Ophelia had answered as she straightened. 'So you don't wander onto it by mistake.'

'...Right.'

I hadn't yet used it, except once to test that it worked. My apprenticeship would be confined to Tuesdays, except when I was out on assignment. We're beginning next week.

After Ophelia left, my apprehensions reached such a height that I spent a full thirty-six hours out in the unicorn glade with Addie. Human doubts and fears don't strike you the same way when you have hooves, a horn and a tail. I recommend it.

They all came flooding back, though, as soon as I regained my human shape. I felt bowed down under the weight of it, as though with my human hands and face and feet I'd also donned a heavy mantle of doubt.

I resigned myself to an unquiet couple of weeks.

Worse, I couldn't even impose on Jay. Not that I should, of course. I've been making all kinds of resolutions in that direction of late; something about *not* behaving as though Jay is there for my personal convenience (even if he does call himself my sidekick). Jay has enough stuff of his own to deal with; he doesn't deserve to have to support me through so much of mine.

Whether or not I can manage to stick to this praiseworthy resolution will have to go a little longer untested, for when I next saw him, he'd donned jacket and boots, and carried his motorcycle helmet in one hand. I bumped into him in the corridor outside my room; apparently he'd been on his way to see me.

'Ves,' he said with a smile. 'I just came to let you know I'm out for a bit.'

'Oh!' I said brightly. 'That's great. Where are you off to?'

'Family time.'

I nodded. He looked all set to go, and a certain restlessness about him suggested he was eager to be off. I confined my response to some murmured platitudes, and waited for him to be gone.

But he stood dithering.

'I've got sort of... well, a date,' he said.

'Oh!'

'I suppose you could call it that.'

'*Are* you calling it that?'

'I mean... that's the idea. Yes.'

'But...?' I ventured, sensing a further hesitation.

'Erm, it's of an unusual kind,' he said, not quite meeting my eye. 'She's the daughter of a friend of my parents. We knew each other pretty well as kids, and... well, I met her again several weeks ago.'

'And hit it off,' I said, beaming. 'Great!'

'Something like that.'

Jay looked fabulously uncomfortable, and I really couldn't figure out why. 'I'm sure you'll have a great time,' I enthused, possibly overdoing the delight just a bit.

He shrugged. 'Our parents would be — I mean, they're really into the idea, and...' He shrugged again.

Why Jay was going into so much detail was as incomprehensible to me as his palpable discomfort. A frown was gathering upon my brow, which I hastily smoothed out. It wouldn't do to seem displeased. 'Are you okay?' I said.

'Yes!' he said, flashing a megawatt smile. 'I'm great. It'll be great, I'm sure.'

'Sure it will. I bet she's lovely.'

'Hope so,' said Jay, so softly I almost didn't catch it. He cleared his throat. 'You'll be seeing Alban?'

'Not to my knowledge.'

'Aha.' He nodded. I wondered if that was either approval or relief I detected in his mostly impassive face, and gave up the attempt. The finer points of Jay's inner feelings are too hard to read. 'Something else?' he said.

'I beg your pardon?'

'Are you doing something else?'

'Not really. Just waiting to get started with Merlin. Might see if I can find out how Orlando's getting on with the argent. You know.'

'Work, then.'

'Always.' I smiled.

'Ves. Don't you ever leave Home?'

'All the time,' I said, frowning again. 'You're usually with me.'

'I mean, for reasons other than work.'

'Of course I do. Loads.'

'Such as that time you...?'

I thought and thought, but failed to recall a single recent incident that wasn't essentially work-related. Even that time we'd hared off at my mother's request had been more to do with my Society position than my status as her daughter. 'Well, maybe I haven't in a while, true.'

'How about ever?'

I folded my arms, a defensive gesture if ever I saw one, but I couldn't help it. It was done before I was aware. 'Just what are you getting at?'

He held out a pacifying hand. 'Nothing. Sorry. I'm not trying to be critical. It's just that I...'

'Yes?' I said.

'...wonder if you're happy. That's all. And now that you're to be taking on a challenging new role...'

'Of course I'm happy,' I said instantly. 'I love my job. I love the Society.'

'Most people have more than just work.'

'Most people don't have *my* job,' I countered. 'It has everything I need.'

'Right.' He nodded.

'I may not have family gatherings, or siblings, or parents who set me up with the hot offspring of their friends, but I don't need that stuff. I've got House, and everyone in it.'

He nodded again, but instead of responding to my litany of self-justification, he said: 'Sometime, I'd... I'd really like you to meet my family.'

I blinked. 'What?'

'You've already met Rina and Indira,' he rushed on. 'You'd really like Anaya and Dev, I promise, and they'd love you. So would my parents.'

'Jay...'

'There's Diwali in the autumn and we'd love you to join us.'

'Are you... are you trying to share your family with me?'

He grinned sheepishly. 'Not exactly?'

'I hope this isn't a pity party.'

'Pity? Never.'

I nodded cautiously, aware that I was eyeing him with deep suspicion.

'It's just a thought,' he said. 'Think it over.' He clapped me awkwardly on my upper arm and took off, his gait super casual.

'Thank you,' I called after him. 'Have a great date.'

Jay waved without turning around. In another instant, he'd turned the corner and vanished beyond sight.

It was my turn to dither. I thought about visiting Val, but I'd bothered her enough lately. She had work to do. Plus, since I had as yet failed to secure the grimoire for her, I wasn't sure I was up for another grilling on that subject.

I suppressed an unworthy urge to text Alban, and angle for an invitation. Jay's observations had bothered me a bit, for all that I'd denied every one of them. And if he was going to have a date, well… couldn't I have one, too?

Not with the married prince of Mandridore. No. I stood with my phone in hand for two minutes, finger hovering over Alban's number, before resolutely putting it away and striding off.

I didn't have any particular destination in mind, but two things happened on the way to nowhere.

The first was a bounding bundle of dandelion fluff, butter-yellow and yipping with delight.

'*Pup!*' I squealed, scooping her up, and burying my face in her soft fur. She's been scarce since Miranda came back, and I've resented that a bit. But I haven't interfered. Whatever my personal feelings about Miranda, I know she takes the best possible care of Pup. Probably better even than I do.

I heard Miranda's voice, then, from somewhere at the other end of the corridor. 'Ah, good, she found you,' she said. 'Jay thought you might like to see her.'

A tiny tear prickled behind my eye. *Jay* had arranged this?

'Have you missed me, you bad Pup?' I whispered into her fur. She certainly behaved as though she had; she was squirming with joy, and doing her best to lick my ear, my nose and my eyeballs all at the same time.

'Thanks,' I called, just as Miranda darted away again. She'd looked almost as uncomfortable as Jay, and that was definitely a hasty retreat she'd beaten. A faint sensation of guilt added itself to the roiling mess of my emotions. I'd made my resentment towards Miranda so obvious, she wouldn't spend more than two minutes in the same room with me.

And I still didn't really feel like I wanted her to.

Sighing, I set Pup down and proceeded on my way. Things certainly looked more positive when I had Goodie Goodfellow frisking along at my heels, and I sent Jay a silent thank you. This girl he was seeing had better be amazing.

I wandered along aimlessly, my thoughts far from Home, until at length I was halted by the sound of someone saying my name.

It was Rob. I'd ended up at the sanitorium. The door stood open, and there he was, on doctor duty today and smiling a welcome at me. 'Morning,' he said. 'Were you coming to see me?'

I hesitated. 'You know what,' I said. 'I think I was, yes.'

In went Pup and I. I took the plain pine chair he offered me, and Pup promptly jumped into my lap. She stood there, wiggling furiously as her tail wagged, and as I bent to pet her she barely avoided stabbing out my eye with her pointy horn.

'You spoke of my maybe seeing Grace,' I said, not looking at Rob. 'A bit ago. Is... is that offer still open?'

'Anytime,' he said. 'I can call her today and tell her you're coming.'

I nodded my assent.

'Right.' He scrawled a quick note for himself, then sat back and surveyed me with his measuring gaze. 'Anything I can do for you?'

I felt the warning prick of tears again, and could almost have immolated myself with frustration. Damn it, when had I turned into this weeping mess of a person?

'It's just tiredness,' I said thickly. 'And — and I'm a bit overwrought. It will go away, won't it?'

He nodded with all the confidence I could wish for. 'It's natural enough. And considering the time you've had lately, I'd be surprised if you weren't feeling unsettled.'

Unsettled. That was a word I could accept. It sounded normal and transitory, and not as though I was losing every shred of my gumption.

I took a breath. 'Maybe we could talk?'

'Of course.' He got up and closed the door, shutting all my challenges and obstacles, potential failures and gnawing fears on the other side of it. In here, just for a little while, I didn't have to face any of them.

'Tell me how you're feeling,' Rob said, and I was struck again by how easily this man could go from grim, Scary Rob to patient and kind-hearted doctor.

How I loved my Society.

'I think it started back in Vale,' I began. I took a deep breath, and the words flowed and flowed. It was a long time before I stopped talking.

But Rob listened and counselled, and Pup wriggled and cuddled, and by the time I left the sanitorium the tears had receded and I felt much more balanced.

Onward, Ves, I told myself sternly. *We can do this.*

With Goodie at my heels, I trailed back to the first-floor common room and took my usual seat. Jay's opposite chair sat empty and dreary, but one thing was there to welcome me: Milady's silver chocolate-pot, pouring steam from the spout.

'Thanks, Milady,' I murmured, pouring a cup. 'We're going to be okay.'

Also By Charlotte E. English

Modern Magick

The Road to Farringale

Toil and Trouble

The Striding Spire

The Fifth Britain

Royalty and Ruin

Music and Misadventure

The Wonders of Vale

The Heart of Hyndorin

Alchemy and Argent
The Magick of Merlin
Dancing and Disaster

House of Werth

Wyrde and Wayward
Wyrde and Wicked
Wyrde and Wild